That's It In A Nutcracker

Jennifer Nice

First published in Great Britain in 2021 by
Write Into The Woods Publishing.

ISBN 978-1-912903-36-8

Cover design and typesetting by Write into the Woods.

www.writeintothewoods.com
www.nicebycandlelight.co.uk

Other Books By
Jennifer Nice

Merry Christmas Eve Eve
That's It In A Nutcracker
All's Fair In Love And Christmas

The Idea Of You

Find them all at
www.nicebycandlelight.co.uk

One

Beth's teeth ached by the time she pulled the car to a stop. Pulling up the handbrake, she took a deep breath, released her jaw muscles and centred herself. This was the part she hated. Every bump in the road had been agony, every turning had been with bated breath. Beth geared herself up and stepped out of her car, slamming the door behind her. Tentatively, she opened the boot and took away the cardboard walls she'd erected, along with the polystyrene padding and bubble wrap. Gradually, the tiers of the white wedding cake were revealed and Beth sighed in relief at the sight of them safe and sound. Leaving the cake where it was and locking her car, Beth went in search of the wedding planner. Through the grand entrance of the hotel, decorated beautifully with ivy and holly, and straight up to reception. They found the wedding planner who introduced himself as Simon and then helped Beth carry the cake tiers, stand and props into the main reception room.

'There's something wonderful about a Christmas wedding,' said Beth as she started putting the cake together. Simon stood over her, hands on his hips, eyes distant.

'Yeah.'

Beth glanced up at him.

'Everything okay?'

The wedding planner blinked and looked down to Beth.

'Yes, yeah. Sorry. This one's been a bit stressful.' He sighed. 'They're all stressful but the Christmas ones more so.' His eyes grew distant again. 'I never used to find them this bad.'

Beth waited but when he didn't continue, she turned back to the cake. The tiers were in place and she carefully added the white roses, a cascade of iced snow and a dusting of edible gold. Simon focused and grinned.

'That's beautiful.'

'Thank you.' Beth reached into her box of tricks and pulled out a business card that had been languishing there since she'd ordered them. The pile was getting low but it wasn't quite time to order more yet. 'Do you want my card? In case you have any other weddings down this way in the future? Flour Power Bakery. I'm on the high street.'

Simon took the card with some reluctance.

'Thanks but, to be honest, this might be my last wedding.'

'Oh? How come?'

'Sort of sick of organising weddings for other people,' Simon mumbled.

Beth did a double take at him.

'I get that,' she murmured. 'Always the baker, never the bride.' She gave a shrug. 'My friend's an event planner, if you ever want to hand anything over to someone else. I'd be happy to put you in touch. She's been talking about organising weddings. Keeps asking me to go into business with her.'

The wedding planner gave Beth a look.

'Why haven't you agreed?'

Beth gave the cake a final flourish and stepped back.

'Because I know how stressful wedding planning can be. You're not the first wedding planner I've met.'

Simon laughed and then checked the time.

'Speaking of which,' he murmured.

'Are you local?'

'No, I'm based in London. But the bride is from around here and this is a lovely venue.'

Beth nodded.

'If you fancy coming back out this way, my friend is organising a Christmas fair and baking competition this year. She used to do tours up at the Manor – that big house on the hill? – but the owner passed away a year ago. So no more tours, but the bakery competition and fair entry is for charity. Everyone's welcome. If you want to meet her or just fancy taking some time out shopping, getting in the Christmas mood, you should come along.'

'Are you entering the competition?'

Beth smiled.

'No, I can't. I've been asked to judge, but I'll have a stall so there'll be some of my stuff available. It's all for a good cause. All the proceeds, and I mean nearly every penny as none of us are getting paid for it and we're getting the venue for free, so everything's going to a homeless charity. The old man who used to own the Manor left it to his youngest son, it's a charity close to his heart.'

Simon raised an impressed eyebrow.

'How did your friend get the venue for free? Out of the goodness of his heart?'

Beth barked a laugh and crossed her arms, giving the cake one last going over with her sharp eyes.

'You could say that. They got together last Christmas and they're both smitten. She moved in a few months ago. He couldn't say no to her running an event from their home at Christmas and she couldn't say no to his choice of charity.'

Simon gave a deep sigh.

'Lucky them.'

Beth's smile faded.

'Yeah.'

A silence fell over them until the wedding planner's phone beeped.

'That's the bride. I best go. Thank you so much for the

cake, it's beautiful. And maybe I will check out this charity event of your friend's. If nothing else, it's a trip out of the city.'

Beth gave him a smile.

'I hope the wedding goes well.'

'Me too,' said Simon with a laugh before turning away and almost running out of the room. Beth made her exit at a slower amble, enjoying the twinkling fairy lights decorating the room and the tall Christmas tree in the corner. Wandering through the bar, she became distracted by the soft Christmas carols playing over the chatter as she weaved through the wedding guests arriving. Turning into reception, she gave a gentle *oof* and looked up into familiar brown eyes.

'Sorry,' she said automatically.

He took a second longer, recognition lighting up his features as he smiled and then apologised.

'I didn't know you knew the bride or groom?' Glen Hargreaves asked, his gaze flitting over Beth in her floury jeans and baseball cap, her coat covering the mess beneath. He frowned and met her eyes again.

'Oh yes, I come to every wedding like this. I never want to upstage the bride,' said Beth with a grin, holding out her arms to give him a better view of her outfit. As his frown deepened, she gave a chuckle. 'I'm just delivering the wedding cake,' she explained.

Glen's frown vanished, replaced with a smile.

'Oh, of course. Wonderful. I can't wait to taste it.'

There was a tantalising moment as they stared at one another, Beth frantically trying to work out what a normal person in a normal situation would say next.

'Are you friends with the bride or groom?'

'The groom, strangely,' said Glen, glancing behind her into the bar.

'Strangely?' asked Beth. 'How strange?'

Glen's eyes met hers again and this time they softened. Something shifted inside Beth.

'I worked with him once in London but she's the one from round here, although we hadn't met before. Small world, huh?'

'Yeah. Small world.' Beth caught herself looking at his lips and ripped her gaze back to his eyes. She opened her mouth to say more when a slender arm snaked its way around Glen's arm. It belonged to a tall, equally slender woman with long brown hair so thick that it belonged in a shampoo advert. She was wearing a low cut blue dress that brought out her eyes and Beth became acutely aware that she was wearing a baseball cap at a wedding.

Glen looked down at the woman and gave a small smile. There was a pause as the women looked at one another and then questioningly up at him.

'Beth, this is Joy. Joy, this is Beth. She's the wedding cake baker and friends with Eve.'

'Eve?' asked Joy, holding out her hand for Beth to take.

'Jeff's girlfriend. My brother?'

Joy gave an elegant singular nod and turned back to Beth.

'Pleasure to meet you.'

'And you,' said Beth with a dry mouth. She dropped Joy's limp hand. 'Well, I best be going. Can't be bringing down the wedding party looking like this. Have fun.' Without looking back she scrambled around Glen and Joy, heading for the door.

'Wait.'

Beth stopped but didn't turn back immediately. First, she scrunched her eyes closed as every fibre in her body told her to run as fast as she could for her car. Slowly, she pivoted on her trainer heel to look back up into Glen's eyes.

'Fancy a drink?'

Beth glanced to Joy who was checking her reflection in a mirror on the reception wall.

'Oh, thank you, but I don't want to interrupt or interfere or…anything.' Beth stepped back, closer to the

10

door.

'No, no, you won't be. Joy, your friend's here, isn't she?'

Joy nodded.

'Over in the corner.' She waved to someone Beth couldn't see. 'If you don't mind?'

'Of course not,' said Glen, turning back to Beth. 'So, let me buy you a drink. Just one. We've got time before the ceremony starts.'

Beth looked down at herself. She used to dress up for delivering wedding cakes and each time she'd drop off the cake and make it back to her car without seeing anyone but the venue staff and perhaps a wedding planner or one family member making themselves useful. It had been a waste of makeup and fancy dresses. It was never part of the plan to bump into someone she knew on her way out and be asked to stay for a drink.

'Sure. Okay. A small one. And I'm driving so no alcohol.'

A grin broke out across Glen's face.

'Of course. C'mon.' He led the way to the bar and after a moment Beth followed, dragging her trainers into the room filled with dressed up wedding guests.

Two

Sitting at the small table Glen pointed out, Beth watched him go to the bar and order their drinks. He smiled at the barman, his eyes bright, teeth flashing. He had a good smile. It didn't seem fair to bump into him at a time like this. His short, dark greying hair was styled, his black suit was impeccable, he looked like he'd lost weight from his gut but maybe that was the magic of being dressed for a wedding. Beth pulled off her baseball cap, permanently dusted with flour and icing sugar, with a large stain of food colouring, and placed it on her lap under the table. She crossed her legs, squeezing her ankles together in an attempt to make herself smaller.

Glen approached, placing a small glass filled with ice and lemonade in front of her and a pint of something golden for himself. She waited until he was settled, his eyes grazing over her sending a familiar sensation through her stomach. Beth glanced back to find Joy still talking to her friend.

'Joy seems nice,' she said.

Glen followed her gaze, holding his pint to his lips.

'She is.' There was a pause as Glen sipped his drink. 'That feels a little out of place,' he said, gesturing with his eyes to a brightly lit-up red and black Nutcracker on the wall. 'Do you think they forgot to take it down?'

Beth swivelled in her chair to look at it.

'Oh, I don't know. Some people find the Nutcracker romantic.'

'Romantic? It's creepy as hell,' said Glen. Beth laughed to herself, turning back to find Glen watching her. 'You like it?' he asked.

She shrugged.

'Actually, yeah. I've always quite liked the Nutcracker.'

Glen smiled to himself, his gaze intense as he looked over her.

'How have you been?' he asked.

'I'm all right. Busy. How about you?'

'Good. It's been a while, hasn't it. I almost didn't recognise you.'

Beth smiled.

'Well, last time we met I was wearing a proper dress and everything.'

'Yeah.'

Beth looked up into the brown of Glen's eyes. His voice was deep, to match his broad chest, and that one word vibrated through the table to her.

'True. I haven't seen Beth the Baker, have I.' Glen grinned again. The last time they'd met, the first time they'd met, he hadn't been smiling much.

'You would have done if you'd come into the café,' Beth pointed out, taking a gulp of her drink. The sooner she was finished, the sooner she could leave, and while a part of her wanted to stay in Glen's presence, the room was getting louder and busier with wedding guests.

Glen shifted, his smile falling.

'I'm sorry I didn't. I meant to. I was going to pop in to get something for the road but we ended up leaving late. I can't remember why.' He frowned. 'The whole trip is a bit hazy.'

Beth's heart pounded.

'Oh? The whole trip?'

13

Glen met her eyes and for a moment it was just the two of them. Beth blinked herself back into the room.

'Well, not the whole trip.' Glen softened and Beth swallowed hard. 'Do you remember the morning after?'

Beth smiled.

'Not really. I get your point.'

'I remember Boxing Day,' said Glen. 'Really well. It was poignant. I don't think I'll ever forget it. The first Boxing Day after my dad died. It was just like it always was but with this huge hole, this big thing missing.'

Beth ran her finger through the condensation on her glass.

'I wasn't supposed to be there. Your dad had invited Eve every year and she had never managed to go, but he never invited me.'

'You were being a good friend,' Glen told her. 'Moral support, weren't you?'

Beth smiled.

'Eve was so nervous. She said the first time she met you, you were quite scary. Arguing with Jeff, being every inch the big brother.' She glanced up at the greying broad man in front of her as he stared down at the table in thought. He'd never for a moment seemed scary to her. 'I'm glad I was there for her,' she added gently.

Slowly, Glen lifted his eyes to hers and gave the smallest hint of a smile. Beth inwardly cursed herself. When he'd failed to show up at her café the following day, she'd ordered herself to stop thinking about him. To stop thinking about what had been and what might have been. It had been one evening and it had obviously meant more to her than to him.

'Me too,' he said softly. 'You brought those...cookies?'

Beth shrugged.

'Who knows. I bake so much all the time. I'm sure I did bring cookies, it sounds like me.'

'I remember how they tasted. I really should have bought some for the road. I really should have stopped by.

I regretted it, you know, the moment I left the town, when I hit the motorway. Even more so when I got home.'

Lacking anything to add, Beth shrugged again.

'If you hadn't been there, I would have been stuck having the same conversations I have every Boxing Day,' Glen added, his gaze back in his pint. 'With Dad's gardeners or with Wendy. It's not Boxing Day if I'm not arguing with my sister in the kitchen. And I just…couldn't. You know? Not last year. Maybe this year.' He looked up and smiled. 'Will you be there this year?'

'Maybe,' said Beth. 'Eve and Jeff haven't said anything yet.'

'They're still going strong?'

It was Beth's turn to smile down into her glass before she took another gulp.

'I've never seen Eve so happy in a relationship.'

When she looked up, Glen had a faint smile lingering on his lips.

'No. Felt a bit destined, didn't it.'

'Very,' Beth agreed.

'Do you believe in that? In destiny?'

Beth blinked, furiously working out how to answer such a question.

'I reckon so.'

'You do. You told me you do.'

'Did I?'

'On Boxing Day. You moved to London as a graduate and got a job in investment banking, of all things. To work off the stress, you would bake and soon people in your office were putting in orders. And you ended up crying one morning, sitting on your kitchen floor, because you realised you wanted to stay home and bake cakes instead of go into the office. But you got up, got dressed, dragged yourself in only to find your senior manager waiting for you with an order for a big wedding cake, and the cheque he gave you made you quit your job.'

Beth stared wide-eyed at the man sitting opposite her.

15

'You remember all that?'

Colour flushed Glen's cheeks and he looked away.

'It got me thinking,' was all he said.

Beth raised an eyebrow.

'Thinking of quitting your city job and becoming a baker?'

Glen laughed.

'I considered it. Not baking, though. Carpentry. I always wanted to do something with my hands but that was always more Jeff's thing.'

'You should do it,' Beth told him.

He met her eyes for one dazzling moment.

'What could a management accountant of thirty years do with his hands? I tried carpentry. Went on a course and everything. I made a bird house and it was awful. I could have killed birds with it.'

'So, not carpentry then?'

Glen laughed.

'I went back into my office the next day filled with a new appreciation for my job. I think what I actually needed was a holiday. A breath of fresh air. That's what...that's what Boxing Day was.'

Beth studied him.

'A grief-stricken breath of fresh air?'

Glen's eyes hardened, his features turning serious.

'Maybe it was seeing Jeff moving on so quickly. Maybe it was meeting you.' His lips twitched. 'God knows I needed that kiss.'

Heat ran up Beth's body and she subconsciously tugged at her collar, aware of how red her neck and cheeks must be.

'Glad I could help,' she murmured. When she glanced back, she caught Glen studying her with a roguish smile. Her breath caught. He'd only smiled once or twice when they'd first met so she hadn't been able to dwell on it. She'd thought his smile charming but that didn't quite cover it. It was as if he was planning something beneath it all, as if he knew what he was doing to her. Then the smile would fall away and there were no plans, no knowledge, just her fluttering heartbeat.

'I wish I could remember why I didn't come visit you the next day,' he murmured.

Beth shook herself.

'Well, it's all in the past now. A whole year has nearly passed. And you have Joy and I have…cakes to make. People think the summer wedding season is busy but Christmas can be a nightmare. There's mince pies and gingerbread and cookies and fruit cakes that need icing, as well as the usual café stock and Christmas wedding cakes. And now Eve's got me judging her charity baking competition—'

'Oh, yes, I heard about that,' Glen interrupted. Beth used it as an excuse to finish her drink. 'Have to admit, I'm glad she's not doing a ghost tour so close to Christmas. And that she's not holding them regularly anymore. Gave me the creeps. Especially just after Dad passed away. It seemed almost disrespectful. I know, I know.' Glen held up his hands as Beth went to protest. 'He would have loved it. He loved those tours. I know. And I know about the one this weekend. But that's different. It's for Dad, in his memory, which is nice in a way. Still, a charity bake sale, or whatever, feels more correct given the situation.'

'Correct?' Beth cocked her head to the side.

'Yeah. You know, when it was built the owners of the Manor would have pretty much owned this whole town. It's nice that Jeff and Eve are going to do a community event that gives back.'

Beth relented. He had a point.

'That's true. Although the money's going to a London homeless charity.'

Glen shrugged.

'It'll become a thing though, won't it. I know my brother and from what I can tell of Eve, they'll make this a regular thing. Before you know it, the church will have a new roof and there'll be a new community centre.'

Beth smiled despite herself.

'That's Eve all over,' she murmured.

'And you'll be there for each one, making the best cookies I've ever eaten.'

Again, their eyes met.

'You're not coming up for the baking competition, then?' she asked. 'It's only a week before Christmas.'

Glen drained the last of his pint.

'Probably not. My son is spending Christmas with his mother this year, so he's spending the week before with me and the schools haven't broken up yet, so I need to stay home.'

'It's a fair, not a cake sale,' said Beth. 'There'll be stalls of local businesses and a brass band and, yes, a cake sale, but it's a baking competition too. And it's on a weekend. The Saturday before Christmas, just after the schools break up.'

Glen stared at her for a moment.

'I guess I really don't have an excuse, then, do I,' he said.

Beth scraped her chair back.

'You don't have to come just because I got rid of your excuses. I'm sure you have better things to be doing with your son. Last minute shopping or other festive things, right? I didn't mean to tell you what you should be doing.' Beth stopped and took a breath. 'I should be going. The wedding's going to start soon and I never stay this long.' She ran her hands down her clothes, gripping her baseball cap in one hand, pulling her car keys from her pocket with the other.

Glen stood up.

'Okay. Well. Thanks for staying for a drink. It was nice to see you again.'

Beth searched his eyes, wondering if there was anything behind those words.

'It was nice to see you again too.' She meant it. Her heart was still pounding, her palms sweating, but her chest tightened with the realisation that she would have to forbid any further thoughts of him once she left. It was the end of last year all over again, wondering why he hadn't visited, wondering if he was thinking of her, wondering if she should ask Jeff for his number, wondering if she was being stupid.

Except that now she knew. She was being stupid. The man had a beautiful girlfriend on his arm, or at least in the corner of the bar, a full life in London and obviously hadn't spared a single thought for her other than for the cookies she'd baked.

'Enjoy the wedding,' she told him. 'And thank you for the drink.'

'Maybe I'll see you later,' he said.

Beth stopped and turned back to him.

'At Boxing Day,' he added.

Struggling for a breath, Beth smiled and nodded.

'Yeah. Maybe. See you.' She didn't turn back again, walking straight out of the bar, out of the hotel and over to her car. There was no pause as she climbed in behind the wheel, no hesitation to look back. She simply started the ignition and drove away, gravel crunching under the tyres as tears pricked her eyes.

Three

It took eight days for Beth to finally stop thinking about Glen during the quiet moments, for him to stop entering her mind as she iced Christmas cakes, to push the memory of their one and only kiss away each time she collapsed on the sofa after a long day. Eight days and Beth hadn't thought of Glen once, until she realised that by thinking that, she had thought of him.

Slamming her rolling pin onto the counter, Beth swore out loud.

'Everything all right, boss?' asked Pete from beyond the kitchen where he was cleaning the café's coffee machine.

'Yeah. Everything's fine. Sorry.' Beth leaned on the worktop. She'd been so close. What was this hold this man had over her? They'd met once, spent one evening together, shared one kiss. He wasn't anything special. A divorced father approaching his mid-fifties with greying hair and a growing beer belly, who lived in London. Beth had dusted her hands of London a long time ago, she had no desire to go back there but that's where Glen's career was, that's where his son was. No, Glen Hargreaves had nothing going for him other than that smile of his, and Beth knew better than to trust a smile like that. No good ever came of them.

'We just sold out of cookies. Again.' Pete's voice pushed through Beth, bringing her away from Londoner smiles and back to her kitchen with a bump. 'Are we doing any more batches?'

'Nope. That's it. Kitchen's closed unless they want something savoury,' Beth called back.

Pete made a noise of acknowledgement and went to give the bad news to whichever customer was waiting. Beth sighed, looking down at the icing she'd been rolling out before Glen forced his way into her thoughts. Shaking her head, she picked up her rolling pin and got back to work. She had this cake to finish icing and then some cupcakes to finish for an early morning order the next day. After that, she'd get a chance to go into the café and help Pete clean. She checked the time on the big clock that hung on the wall between two large chrome refrigerators. It was nearly five. What were the chances of getting the early night she so desperately needed?

Beth pulled a face, putting her weight into the rolling pin. She'd make the time. Maybe an evening to herself resting was just what she needed to finally get Glen out of her head.

She'd just laid the icing over the cake when her phone started ringing. It was sitting on the worktop, away from the food, so Beth hit the answer and speakerphone buttons with her little finger and went back to work.

'Hey,' she called, working the icing onto the cake.

'Hey,' came Eve's voice. 'Am I interrupting? I mean, I know I'm always interrupting but are you free to talk?'

'I'm icing a cake, you're on speakerphone but it's just me in here. Pete's up front. You okay?'

'Yup. Just going through the Christmas fair checklist.'

Beth sighed. She hadn't even looked at the to do list Eve had given her.

'Okay.'

'Can I come visit? I can help clean.'

Beth hesitated but she didn't need to consider it for

long.

'Yes, please.'

She could hear Eve pulling on a coat as she said goodbye and then the line went dead. Beth smiled. Eve's
relationship with Jeff was finally calming down and finding
some sort of normality. Who had a honeymoon period
that lasted a year? Beth raised an eyebrow to herself but
was gracious to admit that she was only jealous. Everyone
around them had begun to assume that this was just what
Eve and Jeff's relationship would be, but finally she was
emerging from the Manor for activities other than work.
Finally, there was a hint of desperation at needing her own
space. It had been a while since Eve had spent any quality
time in Beth's bakery. Every time they'd met, Beth had
gone to the Manor to eat her homemade scones in the
orangery with tea that Eve had prepared, usually after
fighting Janine, Jeff's housekeeper, for kitchen access.

Beth called for Pete who appeared in the doorway,
leaning against the wall, looking every inch as tired as she
felt.

'Eve's popping round to talk Christmas fair but she said
she'd help out with the cleaning.'

Pete's eyes lit up.

'And you want me to create a to do list for her? Got it,
boss.'

Beth laughed.

'I'm not sure Eve can handle another to do list. I know
I can't. But yes, you can delegate.'

Pete grinned and gave a mock salute.

'We're down to our last three tables and are mostly sold
out,' he updated, glancing back at the sound of the café
door opening. 'Best get that.' He vanished and Beth returned her full focus to the Christmas cake.

She'd started decorating it when Eve appeared in the
doorway.

'Good early evening to you!' she declared, taking off
her coat. 'Pete's already told me what I'm cleaning but

there's customers still around. Shall I make a start? Oh, that cake looks good.'

Beth held up a hand to stop her.

'Thank you, it's for the shop tomorrow, so put your eyes back in your head.' She looked up at her friend. 'It's fruit cake.'

'Oh, in that case I won't go anywhere near it. No chocolate cake around?' Eve glanced around the kitchen.

'Cupcakes waiting to be iced. You can have one when I'm done but you need to do the cleaning first. Consider it payment. Then we can talk about the fair, yeah?'

Eve agreed but hesitated before leaving the kitchen. Beth glanced up.

'You all right?'

'Yeah,' said Eve. 'Are you?'

Beth prickled. Eve had known her too long but even when they'd first met, she always knew when something was bothering Beth, however deep she tried to push it.

'Yeah. I'm fine. Go on, Pete will look after you.'

The Christmas cake was finished and ready for the café tomorrow, and Beth was icing the last three cupcakes when Eve came in and collapsed on a stool in the corner of the room.

'I swear, I don't know what I did to Pete to make him hate me.'

Beth laughed and handed Eve a chocolate cupcake sparkling with gold edible glitter. Eve held it for a while, admiring it.

'I don't think he hates you, I think he just needs a pay rise.'

Eve met Beth's eyes.

'Is he getting one?'

Beth shrugged.

'I'm going to offer him one. I reckon what I actually need is a proper assistant but I don't know if he'd be interested. We'll see.'

'So he could take over the baking for the cafe and you could join me in an events business?'

Beth sighed and aimed her piping bag at Eve.

'No. No, no, no,' she told Eve. 'For the millionth time. Oh, I never did tell you, did I. I talked to the wedding planner at that Christmas wedding a week ago.' Eight days ago actually, thought Beth before pushing Glen out of her head again. 'He seemed really fed up, was talking about giving it all up. So I invited him to the fair, to see if he wanted to meet you. I thought he might want to hand the business over, but who hands a business over to a stranger? I don't know. That's probably why I didn't tell you.'

Eve's eyes had widened as Beth talked.

'That would be amazing, to take over an existing business.' She licked some icing off her finger. 'Is he based here?'

Beth shook her head.

'London.' She started tidying up the kitchen. 'You don't need me to start an events business, you know.'

'I do if it's a food events business.'

Beth gave her friend a look.

'Well, make it a non-food events business then. The ghost tours were good and this weekend's event is all sold out.'

Eve shook her head, mouth filled with cupcake.

'Yeah, it's great but Jeff will only let me hold one ghost tour a year at the Manor. It has to be at Christmas and it's in memory of his father. I don't know, it doesn't feel right doing it without Stan, not regularly. I think that's all over now. Once a year feels right, like a little tradition that's come out of all this.' She swallowed her mouthful and studied the cupcake. 'I'll figure it out. I'm enjoying doing project management at the moment, but it can't last forever.'

'You don't like the company you're with?'

Eve shrugged.

'They're too small to progress, I think. Plus, after a

while all those charts and things are going to get boring. No, I want to get back to events. Maybe I need to speak to some wedding planners.' Eve refocused on Beth. 'I could recommend you for wedding cakes. Would that be allowed?'

Beth smiled.

'I'd be disappointed if you didn't.'

Eve laughed and finished the cupcake in two big bites.

'So, the fair,' she started.

'You'll never guess who I bumped into at that wedding,' said Beth at the same time. They looked up at one another.

'Who?' asked Eve.

'No, no. You're right. Let's talk about the fair. I'll start baking for it tomorrow.' Beth put her hands on her hips, surveying the kitchen in thought. 'I think I'm suitably ahead now but I would like an early night tonight.'

'Of course.' Eve nodded. 'Who did you bump into?'

Beth bit her lip and then met her friend's eyes.

'Glen.'

Eve blinked.

'Glen Glen? Jeff's big brother Glen?'

Beth nodded slowly as Eve's eyes lit up.

'What happened? Did you find some more mistletoe?'

'No. No, he was a guest at the wedding. We bumped into each other as I was leaving and he was arriving. He was with this gorgeous woman and I...' Beth looked down at herself. 'I looked like this, actually.'

'So you looked gorgeous as well. Continue,' said Eve.

Beth flashed her a smile.

'And nothing. He bought me a drink and we had a chat and then I left. He didn't tell Jeff he was in the area?'

Eve shrugged.

'Jeff did speak to him but he didn't come say hello. Probably in a rush to get back to London.'

'Probably,' Beth murmured.

'Jeff hasn't mentioned that he's seeing someone though. I wonder who the woman was.'

'Well, it doesn't matter. Maybe he'll bring her to Boxing Day. He didn't seem to know if Jeff was doing Boxing Day this year?'

'Of course he is,' said Eve. 'It's tradition. And you're invited, of course. But I get it if you don't want to come,' she added quickly.

'Thanks. I might skip it this year.'

There was a pause as Beth finished tidying and Eve watched her.

'So, you talked about Boxing Day, huh?'

Beth sighed and looked back to Eve.

'We did.'

'And?'

'And nothing. There's really nothing to tell.'

'But he bought you a drink?'

'And we caught up. He was being polite, Eve. That's all.'

'Did you want something more?'

Beth hesitated.

'Maybe,' she said quietly. She mentally shook herself. 'Let's talk about the fair.'

'What was the wedding like?' Eve asked, ignoring her. 'Was it pretty?'

'The set up was beautiful,' Beth told her. 'But how could it not be? It was all Christmas trees and twinkling lights and flowers. Hard to go wrong with a Christmas wedding. As long as it's tasteful.'

'Hmm.'

Beth looked up at Eve and raised an eyebrow.

'Thinking about a Christmas wedding, are we?'

Eve's cheeks grew pink and she waved Beth away.

'It was just a thought. It would be fitting, wouldn't it.'

'Have you talked about getting married?'

Eve held back a grin and nodded.

'We have. I've dropped hints about a ring. I just don't know how far it'll get me.'

Beth stepped over to Eve and wrapped her arms around her friend in a tight hug.

26

'You better tell me when he proposes. I want to be in the top five of first people to know,' she whispered into Eve's ear. Eve laughed, hugging her back.

'You'll be the third person to know, straight after my parents.'

Beth gave her another squeeze and then pulled away. They grinned at one another.

'So.' Beth clapped her hands. 'The fair. What did you want to discuss?'

'Oh, you know, what you're bringing, what you need, where things are going, timings.'

'That's everything then,' said Beth.

Eve nodded.

'Yup. Oh, hey, want me to ask Jeff for Glen's number?'

Beth nearly tripped over her own foot as she cleaned the kitchen.

'Absolutely not!'

'Why not? I can ask Jeff about this woman Glen was with. Ask if he's single? I'll definitely check he's coming Boxing Day and who he's bringing.'

'Eve, no.'

'Why would he buy you a drink if he's not interested?'

'If he was interested, he wouldn't have waited a year to buy me a drink,' said Beth, turning off the lights and herding Eve into the café. The floor was sparkling clean, the chairs neatly tucked under each table. Beth scraped back two chairs and gestured for Eve to sit.

'I'm off, Beth. Unless there's anything else?' asked Pete from the corner of the room, pulling on his coat.

'No, you go. Thanks so much.'

Pete grinned and gave them both a strange little bow.

'Good evening, ladies. Don't stay up too late.'

'Night, Pete,' Eve called as Pete vanished through the door and up the street. She turned back to Beth. 'What if Glen has spent the last year thinking about you, unable to get you out of his head, and suddenly there you are. He bumps right into you and finally does the right thing, buys you a drink and then, once again, you slip out of his life.' Eve sighed.

'I think you've been in a happy relationship for too long,' said Beth. 'That's not how life works.'

'It worked for me. I'm mean, not exactly like that, but sort of.'

Beth fetched them bottles of lemonade from the fridge under the counter and sat heavily in her chair.

'We're not all as lucky as you, Eve.'

Four

The early night had done wonders and Beth was whistling as she approached her café and bakery on the high street. The wind had picked up but it was an otherwise dry and quite bright December morning. Today was going to be a long one, with yule logs and cakes to bake for the shop along with cookies for the ghost tour that weekend, getting organised for the fair and—

Beth stopped, her momentum forcing her forward one last step. Outside her locked café door was Glen Hargreaves, peering through the glass. She considered turning and running, and she stopped herself from flattening her body against the hairdressers' window next to her as he slowly spun to look up and down the high street. Glen's features brightened when he saw her. She had no choice but to keep walking, albeit slower than before and without any whistling. Heart thumping, she attempted to return his smile as she drew closer. He wasn't wearing a suit this time, but jeans and a jumper covered by a long black coat, topped with a red scarf wrapped around his neck.

'Good morning,' he said. 'I thought it was about time I popped in for those cakes.'

Beth stared at him and then, because she couldn't help it, her smile became genuine.

'You're a bit early. As you can see, we're not open yet.' She gestured to the "closed" sign on the door.

'No. But the hotel I was staying at couldn't do a proper breakfast, something about their oven breaking, and I seem to remember Jeff mentioning that you do a fry up. Even though it's a bakery.' Glen looked up at the shop and then glanced back to her. 'Did I remember that wrong?'

Beth shook her head, pulling out her keys.

'No, we do a full English but you'll have to wait longer than usual. You know, seeing as I'm not even inside yet.'

Glen grinned and followed her into the café.

'I can go away and come back if you like?' he offered, preparing to take off his coat.

'No, it's okay. Take a seat, I'll be right with you.' Beth hurried into the back, turning on the coffee machine as she passed, and took a while to take off her coat. Gradually her heart rate slowed, her breathing returned to normal, and her thoughts began to make more sense.

What was he doing here?

Should she call Eve? She really wanted to call Eve. Had Eve said something to Jeff?

Beth chewed on her lower lip as she tied her hair back and pulled on her apron. What would happen if she called Eve? They'd argue, in hushed tones, and she still wouldn't have the answers she wanted. No, the answers lay in the café. Taking a deep breath, Beth stepped back behind the counter and began making a coffee for herself.

'What would you like?' she asked Glen who had found a table for two in the corner. He'd removed his coat and was unwrapping his scarf as he looked up at her. 'I've got sausages, bacon, hash browns, toast, beans, tomatoes, mushrooms, black pudding, and we have veggie and vegan options too.'

Glen's eyes widened as she talked.

'Erm, yes please?' he said. 'Not veggie or vegan though. I'm a meat eater.'

Beth gave a singular nod.

'Coffee?' she asked.

'Please. Black.'

Beth worked behind the counter in silence, aware of Glen's eyes on her as she took him his coffee. She placed the cup down without spilling a drop.

'I'll go cook the food,' she murmured, flashing him a polite smile.

'Join me?'

Beth stopped and turned back.

'I mean, if you can. Would you like to join me?' Glen looked away, down at the table, his fingers playing with the cup full of coffee. Beth blinked, glancing up at the front door. There was no sign of other customers and while she had a full day to be getting on with, her stomach was already grumbling from her lacking breakfast of an apple.

'You want me to join you for breakfast?' she asked.

Glen nodded.

'So we can talk. If you have the time. If not, I'm happy to follow you around while you work.'

Beth laughed and immediately caught herself, pulling her lips back down. Glen watched her, bemused.

'Okay. Hang on,' Beth relented, disappearing into the kitchen. As she passed, she paused to turn on the soft Christmas music that usually filled the café this time of year, along with the fairy lights that decorated the panelled walls and large window. Glen looked around, surprised, and then chuckled to himself. Beth watched for a moment and then went to turn the oven on.

While cooking their breakfasts, Beth made the decision to keep the "closed" sign on the door. When Pete arrived, she sent him out to buy last minute supplies. He glanced at Glen, raised his eyebrows at her and left with a smirk on his face.

The next time Beth entered the café it was with a full English for Glen and a smaller version for herself. She sat opposite him and took a moment to stop and appreciate the breakfast she hadn't been expecting.

'This looks incredible,' came Glen's voice. She looked up at him and gave a smile.

'No problem. I hope it tastes as good.'

'I'm sure it does.' Glen picked up his knife and fork and started to dig in. Beth went slower, watching Glen as his eyes closed at the taste of the bacon.

'I'm glad you could finally swing by,' said Beth. 'What are you doing here? Another Christmas wedding? And if so, why am I not doing the cake?'

Glen's chewing slowed as he met her eyes. He swallowed and sipped his coffee.

'Well,' he started. 'This weekend is the ghost tour and I thought Jeff might want a hand. Maybe it would be nice to be involved this year, see what all the fuss is about. Especially as it's in memory of Dad.'

Beth nodded, playing with her food.

'How come you're not staying with them?' she asked.

Glen shrugged.

'I didn't want to impose. They're still very lovey-dovey, aren't they? I'm not sure if it's sickening or…'

Beth glanced up.

'Or?'

'Honestly? I get a little jealous, I guess.' Glen shoved a forkful of food into his mouth while Beth considered this.

'What about that woman you're seeing? Are things not lovey-dovey with her?' Beth inwardly flinched. She didn't want to know the answer.

Glen frowned.

'What woman?'

Beth hesitated. No, she had definitely been introduced to a beautiful woman on Glen's arm at the wedding.

'The woman you were with at the wedding?'

After a moment, recognition flooded Glen's eyes.

'Oh. Her.' He loaded up his fork. 'I'm not seeing her. She's a friend who didn't have anyone to go with, I didn't have anyone to go with, so we decided to go together.'

Beth let that settle for a moment, holding back the

smile that was desperately forcing itself onto her lips.

'Oh,' she said, covering her mouth with a gulp of coffee.

'To be honest, I was quite happy living the single life until Jeff and Eve got cosy together. I'm happy for them, I really am. It's been a long time since Jeff had something like this. Been a long time since I have too.' Glen drifted off, staring past Beth, absent-mindedly putting his fork into his mouth.

'Do you see them often?' Beth asked, taking steady breaths, trying to calm her heart rate. 'Or have you been feeling this way since Boxing Day when they started all this lovey-dovey stuff?'

Glen came back to the room, focusing on her. The heat rose to her cheeks and she looked down to her food.

'No but I chat with Jeff regularly. You can hear it in his voice and sometimes hear her in the background. And then there're the times when Jeff does a video call.'

Beth pulled a face.

'Oh, he's one of *those*.'

Glen laughed.

'He is. He does it for work, when he can't get on site, and it's trickled into his personal life. Eve doesn't do video calls? I would have thought if an architect does them then an event planner definitely would.'

'Well, I don't know about professionally, but personally Eve does frantic calls when she needs to talk, immediately, usually here with cake.' Beth smiled. 'I don't mind. She usually ends up helping to clean or something.'

'I can do that,' said Glen, his voice soft. Beth swallowed too hard, glancing up at him.

'You don't have to. She just feels guilty about all the free cake she nabs off me.' Beth shrugged. 'So, you're helping at the ghost tour?'

'I'm going to try. I've been told to do whatever Eve says.'

'Eve knows you're here?'

Glen glanced up.

'Yeah.'

'And you've spoken to her?'

'Of course. I only arrived late last night. I had dinner with them.'

Beth stared at him, wondering how to broach the subject.

'Are you okay?' he asked.

'Mmm, yup. Yeah. I'm fine.' Beth concentrated on her food. She couldn't just ask the question out right, that would be the perfect way of telling Glen just how much he'd gotten under her skin without Eve necessarily having said a word. No. The only option here was to ride it out. Or change the subject.

She looked back up at him.

'And then you're back off to London?'

'Yeah. Back to work for the last week before Christmas. Kind of wish I could take that week off, seems silly to go back just for five days. A lesson for next year, perhaps. I forgot how much I miss this place, and the Manor. Jeff hasn't changed much yet. I'm hoping he doesn't change it too much. Just the carpets, maybe.' Glen chewed thoughtfully. 'Do you think Eve will change a lot?'

Beth smiled.

'You've got nothing to worry about. Eve loves that house just as much as Jeff does.'

Glen nodded.

'They're sickeningly perfect for each other, aren't they,' he said.

Beth laughed.

'Yup.'

There was a pause as Beth concentrated on finishing her breakfast, acutely aware that Glen was watching her.

'Are you seeing anyone?'

Beth narrowly missed a piece of toast going down the wrong way but was forced to cough anyway. That bemused look twitched at Glen's mouth again before it turned into something that was irritatingly devilish. It suited him more than she cared to admit. She managed to chew her mouthful and swallow properly, centring herself as she did.

'No,' she said eventually. 'I'm not. I'm guessing you're not either if you're taking friends to weddings?'

Glen smiled.

'No. I'm not seeing anyone. I haven't had a serious relationship for a long time. They never seem to end well, do they? That's probably why I went to the wedding with Joy. Casual relationships seem just about do-able.'

Beth swallowed.

'Casual?'

'Yeah. Less chance of getting hurt.'

'I absolutely disagree.'

Glen met her eyes.

'How's your son?' Beth mopped up the last of her breakfast.

'He's good. Doing his exams in the summer, already thinking about university. I'm not sure what I'll do without him trashing my house every other week.'

Beth relented, giving a soft smile. Still, she couldn't help herself.

'He's not the reason you're avoiding a serious relationship, then? He's a young adult now, almost the right age for getting his own heart broken.'

Glen frowned.

'Even more reason to protect him.'

Beth gave him a curious look.

'Heartbreak is a rite of passage,' she told him. 'And isn't it worth the risk? If you can get the kind of love that Jeff and Eve have?'

Glen didn't respond. He watched her as she tidied their plates away, and remained silent, finishing his coffee, as she opened the café and positioned herself behind the till as customers started popping in.

Five

The sky was heavy with thick, iron grey cloud as Beth turned off the country road and her car trundled up the long driveway to the Manor house. The trees that lined the driveway were already decorated with fairy lights. Finding a space next to a small, sleek, black BMW, Beth stopped and stared at the car beside her. It was Glen's. She narrowed her eyes. Or was it his sister's? No, no, it was Glen's. Wendy wasn't here this weekend, or at least neither Glen nor Eve had mentioned her.

Taking a deep breath, Beth stepped out of her car, slammed the door and then jumped, her stomach constricting, her heart leaping painfully. Hand on her chest, breathing hard, Beth cursed Eve and all she stood for. In front of her, at the entrance to the orchard, was a robed figure with long, clawed fingers protruding from over-sized sleeves. Beth stared at it for a moment but it didn't move and, after a moment's recovery, her stomach seemed to agree that it wasn't real.

'Beth!'

'What in the name of Christmas is that, Eve?' Beth turned on her friend as Eve skipped out of the Manor's porch towards her. Eve stopped and followed Beth's pointing finger. She laughed which only stirred the anger in Beth's belly.

'It's a gift from Jeff. Did it scare you?'

'I need new underwear,' Beth told her, joining Eve at the back of her car and opening the boot. Eve cackled.

'That can be arranged,' she said, staring down with glee as Beth revealed trays of shortbread ghost biscuits and some strangely shaped gingerbread cookies. 'Is that…Are those…You've made Scrooge cookies?'

Beth glanced up at the fake hooded figure beckoning them to the orchard.

'Give that thing an oil lamp and maybe they're him,' she mumbled.

'Oh, Beth, I love them. You're so clever.'

Beth smiled, settling back. She'd put more work into those Scrooge cookies then she cared to admit. She bent to pick up a tray and Eve did the same.

'How's it going?' Beth asked as she followed Eve into the house. The foyer was decorated as it always was for these things, with beautiful Christmas lights and the odd fake spider web in the corner. This year's tree stood by the staircase, filling the space and sending Christmassy shadows up the walls. Up the stairs, tweaking the angel placed on top, was Jeff. Beth hesitated but only for a moment. She'd walked in once, carrying a tray of cookies, to find Jeff's father standing on the exact same step, placing the angel carefully on the top of the tree. Jeff was almost the spitting image of Stanley Hargreaves and for a moment there, Beth could have sworn she saw a ghost.

Jeff grinned down at her.

'Hey, Beth. You all right?'

'All good, and you?'

Jeff nodded, happy with the angel, and made his way down the stairs to join them.

'Look at these Scrooge cookies, for crying out loud,' Eve told him, brandishing her tray. 'She's out done herself this year.'

'Amazing,' said Jeff, leaning around the tray of cookies

to kiss Eve's lips.

'Thanks,' said Beth, wondering how Eve got a kiss for simply pointing them out when she'd been the one to do all the hard work. Not that she wanted a kiss from Jeff. Of course, that was the moment that Glen decided to walk around the corner and straight into Eve. He skidded to a stop and held up his hands.

'Sorry.' He skirted around her, his eye catching Beth's.

'Look at these Scrooge cookies, Glen. Isn't Beth clever?' Eve showed Glen the contents of her tray.

'Very,' said Glen.

It was skirting on the borders of patronising now. Beth pulled a face.

'Clever and heavy,' she said pointedly to Eve, nudging her slightly in the direction of the kitchen.

'Oh, boys, there's another two trays in Beth's car. Can you grab them?'

'Sure.' Jeff led Glen out of the house and Beth followed Eve to the kitchen where they placed the trays on the wide, wooden worktops. Janine was cleaning by the sink and a teenage boy with dark hair and Glen's mouth was sitting at the kitchen table, staring down at his phone.

'Good evening, Beth. Is it evening yet?' asked Janine.

'Hey, Jan. Just about. Right, what can I help with?' Beth asked, looking around. 'Are these all going out in the orchard as usual?'

'Yup,' said Eve. 'I just need to dig out the trestle tables. Rob can help, can't you, Rob?'

Eve and Janine both turned to the boy at the table but he was too engrossed in his phone to notice. 'Rob?' Eve repeated, knocking on the table.

He looked up.

'You can help with the trestle tables? Yeah?'

'Sure,' said Rob glumly.

Beth caught Eve's eye.

'Rob, you remember Beth from last year's Boxing Day, right? She's the baker. Look at these Scrooge cookies.'

Beth sighed and waited to see if Glen's son would grace her by looking up in her general direction. He didn't.

'Yeah, hi,' he muttered.

'Hi,' Beth murmured. She turned back to Eve. 'Right, I'll help set up but then I think I need to go.'

'What? Why?'

'You have extra help this year with Glen and Rob. You don't need me.'

Eve searched Beth's eyes while Beth blinked, unsure of how much she wanted her friend to work out.

'Set up in the orchard and see how you feel?' Eve offered.

'Fine, maybe I can get your new orchard guardian to help out too.'

Eve grinned and patted Beth on the arm.

Rob might have been quiet but he pulled his weight, helping Beth set up two trestle tables in the orchard. Beth couldn't help but keep her eye on the fake robed figure at the entrance. Turning her back on him seemed to go against her instincts.

'What do you think of that?' she asked Rob, nodding to the figure. He paused in laying out the ghost biscuits to study the robed statue.

'Pretty good,' he said. 'Made me jump when I first saw it.'

'Yeah, me too. Kinda sweet of Jeff to buy it for Eve when he originally said no more ghost tours here.'

'They are a bit…tacky,' said Rob, stepping back to consider his work before moving a biscuit ever so slightly to align it with the others. Beth watched him.

'I didn't know you were here with your dad,' she said, arranging the Scrooge cookies to match his display.

'I only came up this morning,' said Rob. 'Mum dropped me off. Dad said I should come enjoy the tour.' He rolled his eyes.

'But ghost tours are tacky,' said Beth.

'Christmas is worse,' said Rob.

Beth watched him for a moment.

'Why do you say that?'

Rob shrugged.

'Mum and Dad don't really talk. You think it means you get two Christmases and more presents but actually you just get the same but in two different places. And if you're lucky, they won't argue when they swap you. Mum married Steve last year and now she's pregnant.'

'I'm sorry. That must be hard.'

Rob shrugged.

'I'm leaving home soon, so what do I care.'

Something twisted in Beth's stomach. This was why Glen didn't want a serious relationship. It was as if all the blocks suddenly fell into place to form a picture of Rob.

'What are you going to do when you leave home?'

Again, Rob shrugged.

'Study, get a good job. Only see them at the holidays.'

'That sounds…lonely.'

Rob looked up at Beth.

'What did you do?'

'I studied, got a good job, made sure I saw my family at the holidays.'

'And it was lonely?'

Beth nodded.

'And exhausting. If you do that, if you keep running around trying to earn money and build a career and keep forgetting to replenish all that energy and soul destroying muck with things that you love and that fill you with joy, soon you'll be an empty cask unable to get out of bed. Or out of the fridge, in my case. I certainly couldn't make it to the door. Do yourself a favour and skip that bit. Find a job you can enjoy and fill the gaps in your life with things and people you love. And, if you can, include your family in that. They love you.'

Rob turned back to the biscuits and cookies.

'These are good,' he said.

'Thanks. Please don't say you love the Scrooges. Eve's already said it enough for everyone.'

That earned a smile.

'They're all right. I like these.' Rob pointed to the biscuits that Jeff and Glen had brought in from her car. 'The soldiers.'

'The Nutcracker,' Beth told him. 'They're my favourite too.'

'Yeah, I had a toy one when I was little. Dad hated it.' Rob smiled to himself. 'I've still got it somewhere but I keep it at Mum's. Out of respect for Dad.'

'Well, it's not just you and me who like him. They're a bestseller in my bakery,' Beth told him.

'What's it like? Running your own business?'

Beth smiled at Rob.

'It fills me with joy.'

'That's not really an answer, is it.'

Beth laughed.

'No, it's not. Honestly? It's really hard work. You know I said I didn't get to see a lot of the people I loved before? Well, starting this business, I still didn't get to see people. Not until recently. I still had to force myself to make the time. But after a few years, when the business was established and I could afford to hire some help, everything just fell into place. But then, I'm a baker, I tend to get invited out a lot if I bring cookies and cake. Case in point.' Beth gestured to the orchard. Eve or Jeff had hung a creepy ghost in one of the apple trees and everywhere was lit by twinkling Christmas lights. The tour would end here with a brass band playing while the guests ate the biscuits and drank mulled wine or juice. Janine would appear soon with the mulled wine, if she hadn't delegated the task to Jeff or Glen.

'I don't really know what I want to do yet. Just that I want to be good at it,' said Rob.

'Well, you're good at bakery displays. I love what you've done there. Maybe you're a designer of some sort. Or a baker.' She gave him a nudge and he smiled.

There was a pause as Beth brushed down her hands and did her usual triple check of everything.

'You like my dad, don't you?'

Beth stopped, a chill running over her despite her thick coat and woolly hat. She turned back to Rob.

'Why do you say that?'

'Kinda obvious. You look at him differently to everyone else. He really wanted to stop by the bakery and buy some of your cakes last year. I felt bad about that.'

'Why on earth would you feel bad about it?'

''Cause I'm the reason we didn't,' said Rob. 'I was sick and sort of ordered Dad to take me home. He said he just wanted to stop by but he couldn't. We reckon I ate too much the night before. I was up in the middle of the night being sick.' Rob glanced up at Beth. 'Sorry.'

Beth stared at Rob for a moment as the new blocks of information fell into place.

'Don't be sorry. That wasn't your fault at all. You didn't make yourself sick. Did you?'

Rob pulled a face.

'No.'

'Well then. Just be careful how much you eat tonight,' Beth added quietly. Her heart leapt as Rob laughed.

'Well, I like you,' said Rob. 'And it would be nice if Dad was happy again. He deserves to be happier.' He looked over the displays he'd helped create and then shoved his hands in his pockets and ambled out of the orchard, side-stepping the robed figure as he went. Beth watched him go. A breeze lifted the ends of her hair as the realisation dawned on her that she was alone in the orchard.

'Wait up! Don't leave me here!' She jogged after Rob, squeezing past the robed figure and holding her breath as if being so close to it would bring it to life.

Six

As the guests started arriving, Beth escaped back to the orchard on the pretence of waiting for the band to arrive. Soon after, Jeff and Janine carried the mulled wine, juice and an array of glasses through so Beth helped to arrange them.

'Are you all right here?' Jeff asked.

'I am,' said Beth.

Jeff studied her for a moment.

'You're hiding, aren't you.'

Beth grinned.

'Why yes, yes I am.'

Jeff huffed.

'Bit jealous I didn't think of hiding here. It's a bit chilly, though. Wouldn't you rather come hide in the kitchen?'

'No, I'm okay. I'll help the band set up when they arrive and I'll be here when the guests finish up.' Plus hiding away in the kitchen meant being social with the others and it was nice to just have a moment to herself. Not just to get some time away from Glen and the emotions he evoked but she wasn't entirely keen in that moment to be in the same room as Glen, his brother and his son. Right now she could only handle one Hargreaves at a time.

Janine double-checked that Beth really meant to stay in

the orchard and then she and Jeff wandered back to the warm house. As they left, Beth let out a long exhale and relaxed. There was a wonderful silence to the orchard in the darkness. There weren't many lights on in the house, the main one coming from the large kitchen towards the back, almost out of Beth's view. The other main light source was from the Manor's porch where fairy lights spiralled up the columns of wood and reflected off the holly leaves that made up the wreath hanging on the door. The normal light above the front door didn't stand much of a chance. The low light levels meant that above her head, between the drifting cloud, Beth could make out the night sky and winter stars. An icy breeze moved through the trees, finding its way beneath Beth's coat and hat. Shivering, she turned on the outside heaters Jeff had positioned around the tables. While she waited for them to warm up, she rubbed her hands together, pulling out her gloves and slipping them on. Checking that there was no one around, she jogged on the spot for a bit and then considered the unprofessional temptation to eat a ghost biscuit.

Thankfully that was the moment the band arrived and Beth became caught up in helping them to unpack their instruments and set up in their usual spot. They'd been doing this for a few years now and while Beth hardly saw them throughout the rest of the year, it was a little like seeing old friends. A couple were regulars at her café and she had to smack their hands away from the cookies, grinning at the cheers when she produced a Tupperware box filled with the additional biscuits and cookies she'd made just for them.

They helped themselves to a cup of mulled wine each, with juice for the two drivers, and set up, ready for Lyn, the tour's medium and psychic, to lead the guests down to the orchard. Beth's stomach flipped as Janine, Jeff, Glen and Rob appeared before the guests. Glen and Rob were introduced to the band and everyone found positions at the trestle tables, ready to hand out mulled wine, juice and treats. Beth smiled at Rob as he joined her by the biscuits, checking over his work to see if anything had moved.

'Don't worry, I kept them safe,' she murmured to him.

He gave a small smile.

'You weren't tempted to eat them with no one else here?' he asked.

Beth produced the almost empty Tupperware box and offered him a broken ghost biscuit.

'Always bring extra,' she told him. Rob reached into the box and pulled out half a ghost. 'Take a half Scrooge too, if you like gingerbread.' Rob did as he was told, shoving the gingerbread into his mouth. His eyes lit up and he made all the right noises as he chewed his first mouthful.

'Anyone else?' Beth asked, offering the box around. Janine took a gingerbread Scrooge while Jeff grabbed some broken bits from the bottom. Glen glanced at her and pulled out a shortbread ghost. The last one.

'If you don't mind?'

'Of course not.' She gave him a big smile but he looked away, taking a bite from the biscuit. Beth's stomach dropped and she turned back to the table, putting the box away. Rob was still working his way through his own biscuit but shot his father a look which Beth was probably not supposed to see.

There came the rumble of chatter and then a small shriek followed by laughter as Lyn led the tour guests past the robed figure and into the orchard. She finished the last of her story and then Eve led the round of applause before the band started up and the guests made their way eagerly to the tables of goodies. Beth allowed herself to be caught up in chatting to people, handing out biscuits and cookies in paper napkins over the din of the brass band. It was enough to make her forget Glen as the whole orchard became filled with the sound and taste of Christmas.

'How did it go?' she asked Eve when she got the chance.

'Really well,' said Eve. 'I don't think I'm going to be able to ever stop doing this, am I? Every year. The Hargreaves Christmas Ghost Tour.'

'Maybe one day run by Mrs Eve Hargreaves.' Beth gave her friend a wink and a ghost biscuit.

Eve laughed, eyes widening on sight of the biscuit. She was out of breath as she took a bite. Beth stepped back and studied her.

'You okay?'

Eve nodded, eyes scanning the orchard. Beth followed her gaze as it landed on Jeff.

'You're worrying about something,' Beth murmured. 'What is it?'

Eve sighed and stepped closer to Beth to whisper, 'I have a feeling Jeff might propose.'

Beth leaned away, looking Eve in the eye.

'On the porch? Under the mistletoe?' Beth's heart pounded.

Eve nodded.

'Why? Just because it would be ridiculously romantic? Or because he's done something to make you think he's planning it?'

Eve shrugged.

'I'm not sure. It just suddenly occurred to me that it would be sort of perfect.'

Beth laughed.

'He's not going to, Eve. Relax. Enjoy your event.'

'Why don't you think he will?'

Beth raised an eyebrow.

'Because you didn't tell him to.'

'He's creative. He has a mind of his own. And it's hard to forget our first kiss anniversary.'

'Is it? Because you seem to have forgotten that your first kiss under the mistletoe on the porch happened the day before Christmas Eve and today is not that day.'

Eve sagged.

'Oh. I had forgotten that. And that's Jeff's fault, making

me change the date of this tour.' She sighed heavily. 'Well, there go the butterflies. At least I can relax now.'

'Sorry.' Beth slipped an arm around Eve and squeezed her. Eve threw her arms around Beth and gave her a tight hug.

'It's okay. You've also reminded me why I don't have one of your chocolate yule logs sitting in my cupboard yet.'

Beth laughed.

'I'm making them soon. There'll be one with your name on it.'

Soon Eve was distracted by guests thanking her and saying goodbye. Beth wandered back to the tables to check the supply levels. All of the ghost biscuits were gone and there were only two Scrooges left. Rob had also disappeared, leaving only crumbs behind.

'Do you think people will want those?'

Beth looked up at Jeff as he studied the two gingerbread cookies left, forlorn, on their own.

'I reckon you can have them,' she told him. He gave her the charming Hargreaves grin and snatched them up.

'Thanks.'

'Hey,' Beth called him back as he turned to make his escape. 'I don't suppose you've talked to Eve about getting married?'

Jeff blinked.

'What?'

'It's just that, if you haven't yet you might want to. You know, talk about it. Or think about it.'

Jeff looked beyond her to where Eve was chatting away. Then he smiled, bit the head off a Scrooge and gave Beth a single nod.

'No worries,' he said around the gingerbread.

Beth caught herself grinning as she watched him take the other Scrooge to Glen. Jeff said something to his brother who looked up to Beth before turning quickly away. Beth watched him curiously.

The evening ended quietly. There were no declarations of love, no kissing under the mistletoe that hung on the porch, no proposals. Only happy customers, a tired but content and slightly sloshed band, and an exhausted team of helpers. Eve thanked everyone, gave Beth a hug and invited her in for a drink. Beth made her excuses. She had chocolate yule logs to make. That was enough for Eve to carry the empty trays back to Beth's car and wave her off. Once home, Beth kicked off her shoes, found a box of broken shortbread ghosts in an old biscuit tin she kept on the worktop, poured herself a glass of wine, and collapsed on the sofa to relax and feel the throbbing of her feet. She needed a holiday. A proper couple of weeks off and away from everything, but that couldn't happen until she'd asked Pete if he wanted a promotion and maybe hired another helper. Still, the idea of Christmas Day and Boxing Day off was just about enough for now. She would sleep all Christmas Day morning and spend the rest of the day with her family. Then, Boxing Day would be spent with… Beth tensed. There he was again, forcing his way into her thoughts. Glen Hargreaves. Who had bought her a drink when he could have let her walk away, who had a wonderful excuse for not coming to see her the year before, who had just pretty much ignored her throughout the whole ghost tour evening. Beth savagely bit through a shortbread ghost. She didn't have the energy to figure him out which, in hindsight, was probably why she'd been single all these years.

Seven

'So, what I'm proposing,' said Beth as Pete sat back in his chair, trying to hide the way he was nervously rubbing his hands together, 'is promoting you. I haven't figured out a title yet. I thought you could help me with that. Café Manager perhaps. And then I'll hire someone new and they'll report to you in the café, so you can delegate stuff to them. What do you think?' Beth held her breath.

Pete considered this, pursing his lips a little.

'I'd still be working in the café? But I'd be in charge.'

'Yes. You'll be freeing me up to just bake. You'll be taking the café stress off me. I mean, you'll still have to do some of the stuff you do now but you'll have someone to delegate to, more time off because we should be able to stagger shifts, and more pay.'

Pete narrowed his eyes.

'And you can afford that?'

'I can. Just about.'

'I'd quite like to get into the events side of things,' he blurted, his hand unwittingly covering his mouth in attempt to stop more words.

Beth smiled.

'Okay. Great. In that case, how about Café Manager and Head Baker's Assistant or something? You could, I don't know, be first contact for celebration cake customers and you can assist me with delivery.' Beth paused, her mind whirring. 'And I can chat to Eve. If she does more events stuff, she could hire you too.'

Pete's eyes widened.

'Yes. Please. I mean, yes, I would like that. Thank you.'

Beth grinned.

'Great. Have a think about the job title and I'll draw up a new job description. We'll go over it tomorrow and get it all sorted. Yeah? And we can talk a new salary.'

Pete nodded.

'Thank you,' he said. 'I mean that. You've been so wonderful to me. I really appreciate the opportunity.'

Beth shook her head.

'You've been heaven sent, Pete. What would I do without you? I want to pay you back, both in whatever career experience you want and in actual money. As much as I can. This business wouldn't have been able to grow like this without you.'

There was an awkward moment as the meeting finished and Pete looked like he was about to hug her but changed his mind. She almost went in for a hug but reminded herself that she was the boss and stopped.

The door opened, the bell above it tinkling, and Beth exhaled in relief. Pete jumped, heading back to the till, smiling as the customer walked through the door.

'Good afternoon. Oh.' He turned to look for Beth.

Beth stared at Glen as Glen's gaze found her.

'Hi,' he said.

'Hello. Are you here for those cakes you keep forgetting to grab?' she asked, heading towards the counter.

'Actually, a favour.'

Beth stopped and studied Glen.

'If you have a moment?' he added.

'Sure.' Beth exchanged a look with Pete.

'I'll have a latte,' Glen told Pete, taking off his coat. 'Is here okay?' he asked Beth, gesturing to a table by the window.

'Sure.'

'Two lattes?' asked Pete as Beth went to join Glen.

'Please. Thank you.' Beth shot Pete another look as she sat down. She refocused on Glen. 'What's this favour?'

'These went quickly last night,' he said, pulling a napkin-wrapped parcel from his pocket and laying it on the table between them. Beth frowned curiously. Glen unwrapped the napkin to reveal one of the Nutcracker cookies she'd made for the ghost tour. Beth smiled.

'They always go fast,' she explained.

'I was wondering if you could…teach me how to make them?'

Beth stared in horror at Glen.

'You want to learn how to make gingerbread cookies?'

He nodded.

'In the shape of Nutcrackers.'

'But…why?' she asked.

Glen fidgeted.

'Because…Eve and Jeff suggested I enter the baking competition with Rob. Rob likes the Nutcracker.' His gaze flickered up and then away from her.

'He told me you don't like the Nutcracker. You said he was creepy.'

Glen shrugged.

'It's for him, not me.'

'You want me to teach you and him how to make them?'

'No, just me.'

Those three words hung in the air between them as Pete placed their coffees on the table.

'Okay. I need to make gingerbread so, sure. We can do it now if you want?' Beth blinked down at the drink. Her fingertips were tingling, her mind unable to settle on any coherent thought. Trying to make sense of this man was like working to unravel a knot in a string of Christmas lights.

51

'I can't right now. And I don't want to impose. How about tonight?' Glen offered, sipping his scalding coffee.

Beth nodded.

'Okay. Tonight.' That made more sense. It would give her time to prepare. Her day's list filled her mind along with an impending sense of dread.

'What time would be best?' Glen asked.

'Erm. Eight,' she said apologetically. 'Maybe eat before you come otherwise you'll just fill up on gingerbread.'

Glen's smile did something pleasurable to her insides and she inwardly cursed him. What was he up to?

There was another pause as he sipped his coffee and she stared into hers.

'Were you avoiding me last night?' she asked, not looking up. She didn't want to see the expression on his face, the panic or humour or ignorance. She wasn't sure which would be more painful.

'What? No, of course not.'

Beth risked a glance up and Glen searched her eyes. He tapped two fingers on the table.

'No. I wasn't avoiding you,' he said. 'Eve's good at her job, isn't she. Handled the whole thing like a pro.'

'She is a pro,' said Beth.

'Right. I can see why my dad loved those things so much. The house felt…alive.' A sad smile touched his lips for a moment. 'It's nice that she's bringing that back.'

'It is,' Beth murmured.

'Okay, I need to go pick up Rob but I'll buy some cakes while I'm here.' Glen drained his coffee and stood. Beth watched him, her drink completely untouched. 'I'll meet you here at eight?'

The words slowly sank into Beth.

'Oh, no, not here. Everything will be locked up and alarmed by then. Come to mine, I have everything for making gingerbread there. It won't be a professional kitchen but then I guess you'll be using Jeff's kitchen, right?'

Glen handed Beth his phone so she could write down her address and with one of his devilish smiles, he turned away from her to gaze fondly over the cakes she'd made. Pete hovered over him, waiting to pack up his order. Slowly, Beth stood and took her latte towards the kitchen.

'See you tonight, then,' she managed.

'See you at eight,' came Glen's voice.

By the time eight o'clock came around, Beth had made it home in time to shower, have something to eat and prepare the ingredients to make gingerbread biscuits on a clean kitchen worktop. She poured herself a glass of wine and was taking a sip when there was a knock at the door. Not moving, Beth took a deep breath and steadied herself. When she opened the front door she was met by Glen in his long dark coat and red scarf, a hint of that smile of his and a single red rose. She stared at the rose.

'Hi,' she managed.

'Hi.'

She let Glen in, closing the door behind him. He turned back to her and offered her the rose.

'These are surprisingly hard to find. Not the right season, I guess, but I didn't think a sprig of holly would have done the trick.'

Beth looked from the rose to him.

'Trick?'

His eyes softened, a warm smile spreading across his face.

'A thank you, for teaching me how to bake something which I hope is simple.'

Beth laughed and took the rose.

'Well, thank you.'

'I know a bottle of wine is probably more usual in the circumstances but…'

'But?' Beth prompted as Glen shrugged off his coat and scarf, hanging them up on the coat hook Beth gestured to.

'A single red rose is more romantic than a bottle of wine, isn't it. A bottle of wine can mean a lot of things. A rose is straight forward.'

Beth hesitated and looked back to him, opening her mouth, changing her mind and closing it again.

'Can we go through and sit down?' asked Glen as he watched her battle the confusion.

Silently, Beth led him through her small house to the open plan living room-kitchen. Glen sat on the sofa and patted the seat beside him. Carefully, Beth sat with enough distance to allow her to study him. The rose stem was pinched between her fingers, the single sip of wine sizzling through her.

'I know I've been something of an idiot lately,' said Glen, avoiding her gaze. 'I wanted to apologise. Because you were right, I was avoiding you during the ghost tour.'

Beth sagged, staring down at the rose.

'I don't even know why. Rob chastised me afterwards.'

Beth looked up sharply.

'He did? Why?'

Glen slowly looked up into her eyes. His were a soft brown and if he were to put on that smile in that moment she would have melted into the sofa. Maybe she would have melted anyway, if she had the faintest idea of what was going on or what he was thinking.

'He was talking about you quite a lot today. He likes you. And so do I.'

Beth watched him, waiting for more. Glen looked away, glancing back to the kitchen and the bowls of carefully weighed ingredients.

'We should probably get cooking, right?'

'Baking,' Beth corrected. 'Glen, what do you want?'

'Hmm?'

Beth turned so her body faced him.

'I feel like there have been lots of hints dropped and just when I think I've got this and you figured out, you do something that makes me question it. You kiss me under the mistletoe on Boxing Day after an evening of talking and flirting, and then you vanish back to London even though you said you'd pop to the bakery before you left. Okay, so Rob was sick, I understand that now but you didn't say a word. Then I bump into you at a random wedding and you buy me a drink. I wasn't even a guest. That didn't feel like a normal thing. That felt like maybe it meant something except that then you ignored me at the ghost tour. And the problem is that our kiss on Boxing Day did mean something to me. And honestly, I have no idea if it meant anything to you.' Beth snapped her mouth shut and stared down at the rose still clenched between her fingers. When Glen didn't answer, she stood. 'I should go put this in water. Come on, I'll teach you how to make gingerbread.'

She wandered into the kitchen, holding a vase under the tap and slipping the rose into the water. The vase and rose went onto the window sill, out of the way, and Beth calmly tied on her apron. Glen followed her, scanning the bowls of ingredients she'd laid out. When she glanced back to him, he caught her eye and produced something from his pocket. Placing it on the worktop, he unwrapped the paper around it and revealed a shortbread cookie in the shape of a holly leaf. Beth looked back to him.

'Is that…?'

'One of the holly cookies you made and brought along last Boxing Day,' said Glen. 'I was going to eat it but couldn't bring myself to after I couldn't get to your bakery the next day. A friend of mine offered to preserve it after I told her I was worried it would rot. She coated it in resin.'

'You…coated one of my cookies in resin?'

Glen nodded.

'So I could keep it.'

'Why?' Beth breathed. Her stomach churned, wondering whether she should be freaked out or not.

'As a reminder, if nothing else. Of a lovely evening, of that kiss under the mistletoe.' Glen met her eyes. 'As a reminder not to let someone like you slip away from me so easily again. You wanted me to come visit your bakery, right?'

'Of course.' Beth's hand went to her stomach.

'You wanted to see me again.'

'I wanted you to kiss me again,' Beth confessed.

Glen smiled and stepped towards her. Beth's heart raced, after waiting a year for this to happen, it was almost as if it was happening too fast. She couldn't concentrate, she couldn't focus.

The sound of ringing made both of them jump. Glen hesitated and then relented with a huff, pulling his phone from his pocket. He answered, his eyes hard on Beth. She was still breathing hard but this pause gave her time to think. Did she want Glen to kiss her again, here, in her kitchen? Yes, she did. If she was honest, she wanted him to kiss her hard, to lift her up onto the kitchen worktop, to place his arms around her while her fingers worked through his hair—

'I'll be there in a bit.' Glen's voice broke through the fantasy. Beth blinked up at him.

'Is everything okay? Is Rob okay?'

Glen softened again, smiling at her.

'He's fine. An important client has been trying to call me and it turns out my assistant stupidly gave him the Manor's number. That was Jeff. I've got to go and sort it all out. I'm so sorry.' He gave the ingredients a sad look. 'Maybe I won't enter the competition.'

'Oh.'

'It was really just an excuse to be alone with you,' Glen admitted.

'Oh?'

Glen fretted for a moment. Stay here, willed Beth silently. Forget the client, stay with me. Glen didn't hear her.

'Come to Boxing Day,' he said. 'Eve's probably invited you already anyway but if not then come. Come with me.'

56

A smile forced its way onto Beth's lips.

'Okay,' she murmured, unsure of where the evening had gone wrong, or even if it had gone wrong. 'You could still enter the competition. Here, take these ingredients. I'll send you instructions.'

'Really?'

'Yeah.'

'It isn't quite the hands in a bowl mixing gingerbread that I had in mind,' Glen murmured, their eyes meeting again. Beth's stomach twisted pleasurably.

'Oh, so that was your plan? We can do it another time.' She grinned.

Glen's gaze moved up and down her, taking her and her mucky apron in.

'It's a date,' he said.

Beth helped him take the ingredients to his car and ordered him to involve Rob. She would send him the instructions later that evening. He promised to do his best and there was an awkward pause as he opened his car door and turned back to her.

'I'm sorry I messed up again,' he said softly. 'This is the last time, I promise.'

Beth tutted.

'Don't make promises you can't keep, Glen Hargreaves.'

Her chest tightened as that roguish smile bloomed on Glen's face. He leaned forward and Beth prepared herself. His cheek brushed hers and his lips placed a soft kiss on her skin. For a moment his breath was in her ear and his cologne was in her nostrils along with the scent of his warm skin. His stubble grazed over her and then he was gone.

Beth shivered as she watched his car disappear down the road, his warmth still on her cheek. Unable to stop grinning, she skipped back into her house and let out a joyous *whoop!* as soon as the door was closed.

Eight

The day before Christmas Eve was dark with thick cloud. It was a good excuse to turn all the Christmas lights on, twinkling fairy lights that ran along the top of each fair stall on the drive, in the gardens and the orchard of the Manor. The stalls had tables covered in silver-edged tablecloths upon which different products were displayed. There were cheeses and mince pies, handcrafted gifts of coloured glass and bright wool, a selection of Christmas trees in one corner being lovingly chosen and bundled up for families late to decorating their home, carved birdhouses and wooden toys, oil paintings from a local artist, and a photographer darting around and pausing to capture different moments. Off to the side was a line of tables which had started the fair empty but were now slowly filling up with baking competition entries. Beth kept an eye on them, trying not to see who was entering what but ensuring they were all safe and untouched. Janine was officially in charge of overseeing them. She took each entry and covered it, ready for tasting. The crowds had come early, with some lining up at the gate before the opening time. Eve had gone around and checked all of the stallholders were ready before she opened the gates ten minutes early.

Beth had her own stall which she was manning with help from Pete. He was a better salesman than her, it turned out, so she soon found herself letting him take over so she could grab Eve for a chat or dart away for a hot chocolate. All the while, she kept an eye out for Glen and Rob, but saw neither.

'Hey, wedding cake baker.'

Beth turned until she found the owner of the voice. It took her a moment to recognise the wedding planner but when she did they both grinned at one another as Simon reached her.

'Hey,' Beth greeted him.

Simon glanced around the fair. He had a paper bag stuffed with woollen purchases and he did a double take at Beth's own cake stall. 'This fair is really something, isn't it. Did you say your friend organised this whole thing? I wish this had happened at the beginning of December, I could have done all my Christmas shopping here.'

'Good feedback,' said Beth. 'And yes, Eve Dutton put all of this together. It's impressive, isn't it? She's got a passion for it.'

Simon's eyes were still on Beth's cake stall.

'And she wants to get into weddings?'

'Perhaps. Shall I go find her? And you can have a cake while you wait,' Beth offered. Simon's eyes lit up.

'Perfect.'

Beth introduced him to Pete. It didn't go unnoticed that Pete's eyes widened as he said hello to Simon, his cheeks flushing a little. Beth smiled to herself before telling Simon to help himself to a cake while she went searching for Eve.

'Eve. Eve. You remember that wedding planner?' Beth said in a rush, a little out of breath as she reached Eve in the orchard chatting to a stallholder.

'Yeah? Yes?'

'He's here, very impressed and wants a chat.'

Eve stared at Beth as this sank in and then politely excused herself from her conversation with the stallholder.

Beth led her back to Pete and Simon at a fast walk.

'He's impressed?' Eve hissed.

'Very. Wanted to know if you're interested in planning weddings.'

Eve made a strange squeaking noise and then, out of habit, checked the time on her phone.

'Baking competition starts in thirty minutes,' she told Beth. Beth nodded and slowed as her own stall came into sight. Simon and Pete were deep in conversation and a part of Beth didn't want to interrupt.

'Do they know each other?' Eve whispered, slowing next to Beth.

'Literally just met.'

'Cute.' Eve smiled, digging her elbow into Beth. 'You know, I think there's something about this house at Christmas.'

'You think?' Beth dug her elbow into Eve in retaliation. 'Come on.' Beth approached cautiously. 'Simon?'

Simon turned and smiled at Beth, his gaze landing on Eve.

'This is Eve, the magical creator of this fair.' Beth almost did a dramatic bow to show Eve off but thought better of it, dipping away as Simon turned his full attention to Eve.

'So pleased to meet you,' said Simon, shaking Eve's hand. 'Beth tells me you might be interested in organising weddings?'

'Erm, yes, maybe, I think so,' Eve stammered.

'Can we have a chat?' asked Simon. He glanced back to Beth and Pete as he wandered away, throwing Pete a smile.

Beth caught Pete sighing as he watched them walk away.

'Like him, do you?'

'He was nice,' said Pete, busying himself with tidying the stall.

'Did you get his number?'

'Nope.'

'How come?'

'Because I'm an idiot,' said Pete, straightening the table-cloth. 'Plus he lives in London and I don't fancy commuting for a relationship. Double plus he's gorgeous and probably has a boyfriend.'

'You don't know that,' Beth told him gently.

'Nope. No, I don't,' said Pete, his mouth twisting. 'I should go get his number, shouldn't I.'

'I would,' said Beth. 'But be quick or do it later because I have a baking competition to judge and if we leave these cakes unattended they'll be none left when we get back.'

Eve still hadn't re-emerged thirty minutes later so Beth made her way over to the baking competition tables on her own. Janine was waiting for her.

'How's it looking?'

'Amazing,' said Janine. 'I'm glad I'm not judging.'

Beth smiled, glancing over the entries.

'Where's Eve?' Janine asked.

'No idea. She's talking to a wedding planner I met a little while ago.'

'Oh.' Janine's eyes lit up. 'Did she propose to Jeff?'

'Oh, no, she's talking about becoming a wedding planner.'

Janine's face fell.

'Oh. Right, of course. She'd be brilliant at it.'

Beth looked back into the fair.

'She absolutely would,' she murmured.

Beth helped Janine set up for the competition and took her place at the end of the tables. With a few minutes to go, Eve rushed over, a grin stretching from ear to ear, and apologised for being late.

'How did it go?' asked Beth.

'Brilliantly. Tell you later,' said Eve, taking the P.A. system's microphone from Janine and announcing to the fair that the baking competition was about to be judged. Beth sat back in the chair Janine had provided. A small crowd began to gather, people pointing out their entries on the table. Beth tried not to look, she didn't want to be biased by knowing who had baked what. A couple of regulars waved to her, she waved back but refused to look at the table of dishes.

'Judging begins in two minutes,' Eve's voice bounced around the fair. 'You have sixty seconds to get your entry to the table. Quick now.'

Eve jumped as Jeff appeared by her side, kissing her cheek and then giving Beth a thumbs up. Frowning curiously, Beth gave him a thumbs up back.

'Wait! Hold on!'

The crowd parted a little and Glen, red-faced and panting, came running up to the table with a foil-covered plate. He stopped in front of Beth, flashed her an exhausted grin and laid the plate on the table.

'Sorry I'm late,' he managed as Rob appeared behind him.

Beth smiled.

'Better late than never.'

'I think that's becoming the mantra I live by,' Glen muttered as Janine took his entry. His soft eyes met Beth's and she waved him away.

'Go recover. I can't know whose is whose.'

Her insides twisted, sending a jolt of pleasure down her body as Glen winked at her and then leaned on Jeff. His younger brother led him over to the side where Glen collapsed into a chair and caught his breath. Rob had disappeared but Beth didn't have a chance to look for him. The judging was beginning.

'Let's start the baking competition judging, shall we?' boomed Eve's voice. 'We are thrilled that Beth Adams of Flour Power Bakery, on the high street, has agreed to be our judge. First prize is one hundred pounds and a free celebration cake from Flour Power Bakery. Second prize is fifty pounds and a box of cupcakes from Flour Power Bakery. Third prize is twenty-five pounds and a ten pound Flour Power Bakery gift card. Have I said Flour Power

Bakery enough, Beth?'

Beth laughed and nodded to Eve as a chuckle ran through the crowd.

'Let's begin!' said Eve to a round of applause and cheers.

Beth stood and began at one end of the long line of tables. The crowd watched but were, thankfully, not silent. The Christmas music was still playing across the fair, people were chatting, somewhere someone roared with laughter. Some children ran through the crowds, giggling as they went.

The first entry was a plate of mince pies. Beth tasted one and closed her eyes as something that she hadn't baked filled her senses. It was delicious. This was going to be harder than she thought. The second entry was a plate of white chocolate and cranberry muffins which was strange but somehow worked perfectly. The third was a large celebration cake decorated in fondant to represent a sprig of holly. Beth sliced through it revealing layers of green sponge and white buttercream. She could only take small bites of each thing, which felt like a waste until she saw Janine, Eve and Jeff behind her helping to polish off what was left before the untouched remains were given back to the entrant.

There were more mince pies in different types of pastry, a cranberry pie which was unfortunately more bitter than sweet, heaps of gooey brownies, chocolate logs thick with icing, apple pies that melted in the mouth, wobbly gingerbread houses constructed with love, layered cakes with gold icing and one beautifully designed as a snow globe, cupcakes, biscuits, the variety was stunning. Beth reached a plate and stopped. On the plate were seven gingerbread biscuits that, if she squinted and tilted her head, almost looked like Nutcrackers. Her chest tightened and before she could stop herself, her eyes were up searching for Glen. She spotted him in the corner, arms crossed against his broad chest, his slight belly beneath, and a worried twitch at the edge of his mouth. The biscuits were warped and perhaps rushed but Beth snapped the arm from one and popped it into her mouth.

'Good texture,' she told Janine who wrote down the notes on her clipboard. 'Good flavour. Design is…well, they tried hard.' She kept her eyes on Glen as she swallowed the gingerbread. A smile forced its way onto his face.

'How are they?' Jeff asked quietly.

'Shush,' Eve hissed.

'Oh, come on, she's staring right at him. She knows they're his.' Jeff reached across and took the armless gingerbread Nutcracker from the plate, snapping off a leg and passing it to Eve to try.

In the end Beth had a terrible time of choosing a winner. She wanted to give the family who had built a wonky gingerbread house something but the snow globe and celebration cakes were incredible, not to mention that apple pie. In the end, she bargained with Eve and gave out joint prizes. The gingerbread house came third, much to the delight of the family of five who had made it, a layered celebration cake and a chocolate log took second place and that snow globe and apple pie took joint first place. Beth explained how difficult judging had been and how she hoped none of them got any ideas of starting their own bakery on the high street, then passed Eve the microphone so she could announce the end of the fair.

Beth's body relaxed as she stepped away, reaching for the plate of Nutcrackers and finding a quiet spot to herself.

'You'll definitely need a drink with those,' came Glen's voice. Beth looked up and smiled as he approached with two paper cups of beer. 'You really shouldn't eat them. I was worried about you just taking one bite.'

'Why? They're delicious. You understand why I couldn't place you, though, right?' Beth took the beer he offered and they settled down together on a bench so recently vacated that the wood was still warm.

'Yeah, they're awful.'

'I couldn't be seen to be biased,' Beth corrected.

Glen laughed.

'Oh yeah, otherwise you'd have put them first, right?'

Beth offered him the plate of his own biscuits. He gave her a look until she said, 'Go on, try one.'

He took a biscuit and the smallest bite. His features lightened as he chewed.

'Actually not that bad.'

'No, they're delicious. You just need to work on your decoration, that's all. That's my fault, I didn't teach you any of that.'

Glen watched her silently for a moment, his gaze lingering on her lips. She hesitated, wondering if she was about to get a gingerbread flavoured kiss.

'Does the Nutcracker still freak you out?' she murmured, looking up at him.

'He does. But you like him,' said Glen softly.

Beth smiled.

'I thought you made these because Rob liked him?'

Glen cursed under his breath and then laughed.

'Well, there you go. You caught me. Rob used to like the Nutcracker when he was little but not anymore. Now he prefers cars, guitars and people his own age.'

Beth grinned.

'You made them for me,' she breathed.

Glen searched her eyes.

'I came back for you,' he said, leaning towards her. Beth echoed him and just as their lips were about to touch, her skin tingling with anticipated pleasure, there came the call of, 'Glen? Beth?'

They jumped apart and looked around. The crowd of the fair was dispersing, only a few families were left now along with the friends and staff of the Manor and the stallholders packing away their wares.

'Beth?' Janine caught sight of them and beckoned them over. Curious, Beth and Glen exchanged a glance and stood, taking their biscuits and beer with them.

'We're going back to that moment,' Glen whispered in her ear. Beth's heart thudded as she nodded. They ended up outside the front of the Manor and she made sure she stood just a little too close to Glen so that his arm brushed against her. There was a shuffling and then the feel of his fingers against her back. A shudder of warmth moved through her body.

Jeff had Eve's hand and was leading her over to the porch, glancing around at the small crowd.

'Eve,' he started, clearing his throat and wringing his hands after he positioned her on the porch. Eve was staring at him with wide eyes. It dawned on Beth what was about to happen and she shoved the plate of Nutcrackers into Glen's hand so that she could cover her mouth and keep her reaction in. 'Eve, almost exactly a year ago to the hour we stood here, on this porch, under a sprig of mistletoe and had our first kiss. The last year has been…' Jeff sighed, biting his lip against the grin. 'Magic. Because you are magic. You brought magic into my father's life, you brought it into this house and now you've filled my life with it. And I don't want that to stop. Ever. I want my life to be filled with your magic and I want to make you as happy as you've made me. I want to be here for you as you've been here for me.'

A quiet gasp ran through the crowd as Jeff got down on one knee.

'Eve Dutton, will you marry me?'

Beth was bouncing on the balls of her feet, something she only became aware of when she realised Glen was watching her and not his brother's proposal. Beth resisted the urge to look up at Glen, keeping her eyes on Eve as her friend nodded and wrapped her arms around Jeff's neck. The crowd cheered and applauded as Jeff swung Eve round, lips pressed against hers. When Jeff let her go, Eve squealed and searched the crowd for Beth. Glen took

Beth's beer so they could run towards each other. Beth held Eve tight.

'Finally,' she murmured. Eve giggled.

'You'll make the cake, right?'

Nine

Beth had spent Christmas Eve and Christmas Day too busy to think but even so, whenever she stopped, the thought of Glen would push its way through. Glen and that near kiss. Glen and his gingerbread Nutcracker biscuits. Glen and his broad frame and the sense of safety whenever he was next to her. When her mother had suggested she stay for Boxing Day, she'd been forced to tell her everything. Her mother had smiled, hand over her heart, and told Beth she had to go to the Manor for Boxing Day. Beth promised she'd spend the following week back with her family, packed her bags and popped home for a shower and change of clothes before rushing up to the Manor.

This time last year, she'd walked into the Manor behind Eve wondering what on earth she was doing. She'd brought mince pies and biscuits, been introduced to Jeff's family, and there had been a soft silence in the house as they'd mourned Stanley Hargreaves. His father's death had hit Glen hard and he'd been in no mood for talking when Beth had first attempted to start a conversation. She'd ended up watching the television with Rob instead until she caught Glen swooning over her mince pies. That had been the ice breaker she'd needed to engage in adult conversation and once Glen had a couple of mince pies and a few glasses of wine in him, he'd begun to open up. No wonder they'd ended up underneath the mistletoe on the porch, watching their breath cloud against the cold air as they took a break from being surrounded by people.

Beth hesitated as she went to knock on the Manor's front door. Glancing up at the mistletoe, she smiled. She'd glanced up at it on a late Boxing Day last year, somehow at the same time that Glen had also glanced up. Their eyes had met, the world spinning a little as Glen had stepped forward and placed his lips on hers. It had been a somewhat drunken first kiss but unlike any other drunken kiss Beth had experienced. It had been enough to stay with her for a whole year, almost a forgotten, faded memory until Glen had walked around the corner and straight into her at the wedding.

Beth took a deep breath and knocked on the door. Eve answered, a grin plastered to her face and a sparkling diamond ring on her finger which she immediately showed to Beth. Beth did the usual crooning and gasping expected and then passed a box of mince pies to her friend. Eve barely noticed, she was so caught up in the day, talking non-stop about who was there, what was happening, how her day had been, how wonderful Christmas had been.

'Did you have a good Christmas?'

Beth blinked, Eve's words finally breaking through.

'Yeah, it was lovely. I have a Christmas cake here.' She showed Eve a second box that she was carrying beneath a tray of shortbread biscuits.

'Oh, Beth. You spoil us.' Eve, unable to grin further or clap her hands, did a little skip. 'The yule log you made me was incredible. We shared some with Glen, Wendy and the kids, of course, but kept half just for us.' Eve winked.

Beth laughed.

'I don't want to know what you two get up to with my yule logs.'

Eve gave her a playful look and led her through the

house and into the kitchen. As she walked past the living room, Beth glanced through and somehow managed to catch Glen's eye as he peered through the doorway. Had he been waiting for her? Or had he simply heard her voice?

'You never did tell me about what happened with Simon, the wedding planner,' Beth murmured as she walked into the kitchen to find Wendy, the middle Hargreaves child, preparing some roast potatoes. Wendy smiled at Beth in such a way that suggested she knew something. Beth narrowed her eyes.

'Hi, Wendy.'

'Beth. Did you have a good Christmas?'

'Yes, thanks. You?'

Wendy nodded.

'It was...quiet. My first Christmas as a single mother.' She gave a short laugh. 'Jeff and Eve kindly invited us here but I wanted to get that first Christmas over with, you know? It went better than expected.'

'That must have been tough. I'm glad you're here now. Are your kids here too?' Beth hadn't heard the telltale noise of children.

'No, they're with their dad today and tomorrow.' Wendy sighed. 'It's a weird feeling. Somewhere between relaxing and wondering what I've forgotten all the time.'

Beth smiled.

'Well, I've brought mince pies, shortbread and Christmas cake, if that helps?'

Wendy's eyes widened.

'You know, I've been thinking about your mince pies all year. They'll definitely fill the gap.'

Beth looked around the kitchen and then out of the doorway before sneakily opening the box with the mince pies and offering them to Wendy. Wendy glanced at Eve and took one mince pie, biting into it immediately and closing her eyes.

'They live up to the memory,' she said around the mouthful. 'Thank you.'

'Anytime,' said Beth. 'So? Wedding planner?' She turned back to Eve.

'Simon asked if I wanted to buy his business,' said Eve.

'What? No franchise, no joint partners, no delegating to you?' Beth leaned back against a worktop, taking this in.

'Nope. A straight up buy my business deal.'

'How much?'

'Not as much as you'd think. I'd be buying a couple of booked weddings from him, if the clients want to continue, and a list of suppliers. Not including a baker, I told him I have one of those.' Eve raised a questioning eyebrow at Beth.

'You know I'd love to be your go-to wedding cake maker,' Beth told her. 'Especially now that Pete has been promoted. He's told me he'd love to be more involved in the events side, so I know he'd be happy to help and get involved. He hit it off with Simon, I'm hoping he doesn't run off to London now to see more of him.'

Eve gasped.

'That would be amazing. Not for you, obviously.'

Beth shrugged.

'Life happens,' she said. 'You're going to buy the business?'

'I can't afford it,' Eve admitted. 'I can afford half of it.' She drifted off, staring at Beth. Beth blinked.

'What are you saying?'

'I'm suggesting that you buy the other half and we become partners.'

Beth grimaced but then images of wedding cakes floated through her mind. Of all the things she truly loved making, decorating a wedding cake was at the top of her list.

'Maybe,' she said. 'I'll think about it.'

Eve agreed.

'Okay. Sure. Probably the wrong day to ask anyway. Today is for relaxing and celebrating and eating roast potatoes and cake.'

Wendy smiled at Eve, turning back to face the friends.

'You know, Jeff might be keen to invest,' she suggested. 'Or Glen. Glen did a lot of investing in his younger days.' She glanced at Beth. 'Or, you know, maybe I could invest.'

Eve considered this.

'A family partnership,' she murmured.

'Exactly,' said Wendy.

'What's this? What plans are you concocting?' asked Jeff as he walked into the kitchen. Glen followed with an empty glass.

'Business plans,' Eve told him, unable to keep the smile from her face as Jeff snaked an arm around her waist. 'The wedding planning business.'

Jeff looked between Eve, Beth and Wendy.

'That could work,' he murmured, grinning at his sister.

Beth looked sideways at Glen as he poured himself another glass of wine.

'Did I see you come in with mince pies?' he asked quietly, just between the two of them.

Beth opened the box and offered him one.

'But don't tell anyone,' she whispered back, aware that everyone was watching them. Glen laughed and took a bite.

Jeff poured Beth a drink and she remained by Glen's side, unsure of what else to do with herself. The kitchen was full and warm, and eventually Wendy demanded that everyone leave so she could cook in peace.

They traipsed into the living room and there was a knock at the door as Janine, Harry and Dave, the Manor's gardeners, arrived. Jeff and Eve went to see them in and get them drinks, leaving Beth with Glen and Rob, on the sofas in front of the television.

'Turn that off now, Rob,' said Glen. 'Time to chat before dinner.'

Rob did as he was told and there was a silence between the three of them. A warmth spread through Beth's chest as she watched father and son for a moment. This could be it, she thought. This is what life could be like.

The thought was broken by the newly arrived guests descending on them with loud voices and demands for Beth's mince pies.

Ten

After a wonderful meal cooked entirely by Wendy, before Beth's Christmas cake made an appearance, the family and their friends settled back with full bellies in front of the fire.

'No snow this year,' said Harry.

'There's time yet,' said Jeff, his arm around Eve who was slowly falling asleep, her cheek against his chest.

Beth watched her friend, the diamond on her finger catching her eye as it glistened in the firelight. Slowly, she got up and placed down her drink, making her way out of the room.

'Everything okay?' asked Eve, eyes suddenly open.

'Going to the bathroom. If I'm not back in half an hour, I've fallen into a food coma and you're to come wake me up with cake,' Beth told her.

Eve settled back into Jeff's arms, a contented smile on her face as her eyes closed again.

Beth didn't go to the bathroom. Instead, she quietly opened the front door and stood out on the porch. Harry was right, there was no snow and it was too dark to see what the clouds above were like. There were definitely clouds, Beth couldn't see a single star but she could feel the heaviness. She sniffed and wondered if that heavy scent was a promise. Filling her lungs with the chill night air, she leaned back against the wood of the porch, her mind drifting.

'This isn't the bathroom,' whispered Glen, making her jump as he softly closed the door behind him.

'Don't creep up on me,' she told me, hand over her heart. 'Scared the life out of me.'

He smiled playfully.

'Sorry. Next time I'll knock.'

She gave him a look.

'I think the lights are still up around the orchard,' said Glen, peering around her. 'Do you want to go see?'

Beth's heart jumped sending something exquisite through her body.

'Sure.' She shrugged, wrapping her arms around her and stepping off the porch. Glen looked her up and down before vanishing back into the house. 'Or not?' she called softly after him.

He reappeared with their coats and she gratefully pulled hers on. It was one thing standing on the porch by the heat of the house and another walking down to the darkness of the orchard.

'Have you flicked the light switch?' she asked as Glen led the way onto the driveway and over the gravel.

'I have,' said Glen, pausing so she could catch up.

As they walked towards the glow of the orchard, with the fairy lights still obviously up and working, the backs of their hands brushed against one another. Glen's finger reached out and curled around her little finger. Smiling to herself, Beth took his hand in hers and he gave her a gentle squeeze. No words were spoken. Beth wasn't sure she could remember how to form words as her mind whirred, her body tingling.

Glen led her into the orchard and they paused, taking in the sight of the fairy lights twirling up each apple and pear tree.

'We should spend more of Christmas here,' Beth

breathed. 'It's beautiful without a crowd.'

Glen found the bench over to the side and sat, patting the space beside him for Beth. She sat slowly, wondering if she was sitting too close but unable to make herself move away. He didn't seem to mind. They sat in silence for a moment, taking in the lights and stillness of the trees. A shiver ran through Beth as a breeze picked up. She pulled her coat tighter and shoved her hands into her pockets.

'I'll be quick,' said Glen.

Beth turned to him sharply.

'What?'

Glen struggled for a moment and then pulled something out of his pocket. Beth exhaled in a cloud as she realised it was a wrapped gift. Her eyes lifted to his.

'You bought me something?'

He nodded.

'I saw it and thought of you.'

Beth bit her lip as her insides somersaulted. Pulling her hands from her pockets, she took the gift.

'You really didn't have to.'

'I know,' he said, watching her. 'Open it.'

With shaking fingers, Beth clumsily unwrapped the present. It had been beautifully done and she couldn't help but wonder if he'd had it gift-wrapped in a shop. Inside the green and gold paper was a box. She glanced up, smiling. The tape gave way under her fingernails and inside the box, under a layer of tissue, was a pristine and beautifully made glass ornament of red and black.

Beth laughed, looking up into Glen's smile

'You bought me a Nutcracker.'

He nodded as she carefully removed the soldier from the box, holding it up against the fairy lights.

'It's a tree ornament,' he told her, his voice low as if the words were a secret, just for her.

'It's beautiful,' she breathed as the light twinkled through the glass. Her chest tightened, tears pricking her eyes. 'I love it. Thank you.'

Glen leaned closer.

'Will you think of me when you look at it?'

Beth smiled.

'Honestly? I think about you now whenever I see a Nutcracker.' She turned to find Glen's face close to hers. Carefully, barely looking, she placed the ornament back into the box.

'I do sort of wish they weren't called Nutcrackers,' Glen murmured, his eyes on her lips.

Beth gave a soft laugh and for a moment, the tips of their noses touched.

'I sort of wish I didn't have to look at a Nutcracker to be reminded of you,' she breathed back. His eyes lifted to hers. 'I sort of wish I could just look at you,' she added, her mouth dry, heart racing.

The corners of his mouth lifted into a slow smile and he gave a slight shake of his head.

'I don't know what it is,' he said. 'If it's your eyes or your smile or the way you always smell of cake or just the thought of how soft your hands are underneath the flour and icing, but I just can't...' He drifted off, lowering his eyes again.

'Can't what?' asked Beth, holding her breath, readying herself for this to go horribly wrong.

'Resist you,' Glen finished, his eyes back on hers. 'I tried. Kept telling myself I didn't want anything serious, that it's better to just be me and my son, but... He's nearly grown up and I just can't...resist you.'

Beth didn't even try to stop the grin spreading over her face. She leaned closer until her lips grazed over his.

'Then don't,' she murmured.

'Come to London with me,' he said, the words spilling out fast in an exhale. She searched his eyes, the tips of their noses bumping again.

'Sometimes,' she agreed. 'If you come here sometimes and take me away from my kitchen.'

Glen smiled.

77

'I can work with that,' he murmured. One of his arms had moved around the back of her and now lay gently against her lower back and waist. 'We'll work it out.'

'Promise,' said Beth without thinking, her eyes already closing.

'Promise,' said Glen as his lips met hers.

The kiss was soft at first as they felt their way. Then it deepened, became a little harder. Glen took the gift from Beth's lap and placed it at their feet before wrapping his arms around her. Her hands were in his hair, holding him close. The scent of his cologne filled her senses, along with the tingle of his warmth against her chill, the tenderness of his lips, the feel of his slight stubble as her fingers brushed over his cheek.

As they parted, Glen kept his arms around her and Beth let one hand slide down his arm. He watched her and she wondered if they were thinking the same thing. He took her hand in his, rubbing her cold fingertips.

'We should do that more often,' he said.

She nodded.

'We should.'

'I'm sorry I didn't do that a year ago.'

'You did,' Beth pointed out. 'On the porch, under the mistletoe.'

Glen sighed.

'Copying my brother.' He looked down at their entwined hands. 'Because I wasn't sure what else to do. This is more me.' He glanced around the orchard.

'And me,' said Beth. Glen looked back to her.

'I don't have to stay in London for work,' he told her.

'We can figure it out,' she assured him.

'And I won't be proposing to you here on this spot in a year's time.'

'Oh?'

'No. It'll be somewhere different, when you're not expecting it.'

Beth laughed and Glen lifted her hand and pressed it to

his lips.

'Beth? Glen? Are you out here?' Eve's voice made Beth flinch, her grip on Glen tightening. She looked at him with widening eyes. 'Cake time!' Eve called.

'Well, going back in is going to be awkward,' Beth told Glen with a smile. 'I reckon they all know where we've been.'

Glen searched her eyes.

'Let's stay out here a little longer then,' he told her, pulling her closer.

'You don't want any cake?'

Glen gave a slight shrug.

'I'm hoping that one of the benefits of this happening is that I don't have to wait until Christmas to eat cake made by you.'

Beth grinned as her mind settled, that pleasant, tingling warmth spreading throughout her entire body until it reached her fingertips. She put her arms around Glen's neck and moved forward for another kiss.

Just before their lips met, something cold and wet hit her head. They both looked up.

'Can't be,' Glen murmured.

Beth held out her hands and then looked up at him.

'Do we go in and tell them it's starting to snow?'

Glen's eyes twinkled in the fairy lights.

'Nah.' He leaned in, pulled her close and kissed her as she smiled against his lips. Let the others find them. For now, this was their world. Just the warmth of one another, a glass Nutcracker, twinkling lights among the fruit trees and the first snowflakes of the season.

***

Acknowledgements

This story came about after a Christmas spent discussing with my mum how magical yet very creepy the Nutcracker image is.

After reading this book, she immediately bought me a Nutcracker tree decoration.
Thanks Mum!

Thank you to my husband and dad for putting up with me working on/talking about Christmas romance all the time. I take full blame for my husband walking around the house humming Christmas songs in August.

A big thank you to Vicky at Tallulah's Bakery (@tallulahsbakery) for her hilarious Instagram reels about how to transport a cake and her advice on how Beth should keep the wedding cake safe in the car. (Check out her fondant cakes – she could teach Beth a thing or two.)

Turn the page for a sneak peak
of the next book in the series.

All's Fair

In Love and

Christmas

Available now from www.nicebycandlelight.co.uk

One

Looking at the time had become less of a habit and more of a compulsion. Wendy had one hour to go before she had to leave the office to pick her children up from school. One hour. She could get a lot done in an hour. Then she'd leave the office and make her way back to her car, parked a short Tube ride away. After picking the children up, she'd make them something to eat and sort out her daughter's homework. Her son needed socks. She mustn't forget the socks. His Christmas bag still needed packing. Wendy always had to time packing his bag otherwise he'd empty it and wear everything just before going to his father's. The divorce had been the right thing to do but sometimes she remembered a simpler life when there weren't so many bags to pack. A couple of years ago, two weeks before Christmas, Wendy had been sitting in this chair, at this desk, contemplating Christmas presents and buying a tree. This year she was that woman who walked into the Tube station muttering, 'Socks,' under her breath.

She sighed and checked the clock.

Fifty-five minutes to go.

'Wendy? Can I have a moment?'

Wendy hid the jump of fright well, she thought. She smiled up at her boss and stood, following him into his office. She closed the door behind her and sat opposite him, his desk between them. There was always that moment of anxiety before he spoke. Why had she been summoned? Was this about the promotion? Was he about to promote her now?

'Are you all ready for Christmas?' Graham asked nonchalantly. He was around fifteen years her senior and while he would say his hair was pepper flecked with salt, it was definitely now more salt than pepper. His fingernails were short from where he bit them, something that had driven Wendy mad when she'd first joined the firm. Sitting in a meeting with a client next to a man who bit his nails had slowly become infuriating. It was a bad habit, he told her once, that had replaced the worse habit of smoking. After that, she didn't feel able to complain about it.

'Yes. Getting there,' she told him.

He nodded, tapping at the desk. The man always needed something to keep his hands busy. She watched distractedly. When was he going to get to the point?

'I think I'm actually going to have Christmas off this year.' Graham gave something of a laugh. 'We'll have filled the partner position by then, so I'm hoping we can all relax a little.'

Wendy nodded. Yes, the partner position. Is that why she was here? It was why she was here generally, in the building. It was why she'd taken this role. Just over ten years spent working cases, paying her dues, all so that she could make partner. This was going to be her year. It had to be.

'Claire's booked us a holiday. Which will be nice. Skiing. I can't stand it but I do like the idea of relaxing with a brandy surrounded by snowy mountains over Christmas.'

Wendy nodded again. Smile and nod, smile and nod, get on with it, man!

'The kids are happy but she left it late to book. It's been expensive.' Graham sighed. 'Do you have your kids this year?'

Wendy shook her head.

'With their father this year?' he continued before she could open her mouth. 'Divorce is a bitch. I should know, I was a divorce lawyer when I started out. Did I ever tell you that?'

Wendy nodded.

'You did,' she said. Multiple times, usually while a bit tipsy at the office Christmas party. He'd offered to help her when he'd heard about her divorce but she preferred to keep the whole thing out of the office.

'Do you have Christmas plans without them?'

'I'm going to my brother's,' said Wendy. 'He owns our old childhood home now—'

'Oh, that glorious old house out in the sticks?' Graham interrupted.

'Yes—'

'Wonderful. That sounds very festive. And relaxing, I hope? Does he have children?'

Wendy shook her head.

'No, he—'

'Nice and relaxing,' said Graham.

Wendy sighed inaudibly. Usually she'd put up a fight when Graham got into this state of cutting her off. Usually she'd call him on it, tell him to get on with it, tell him to let her get a word in. Usually she'd stick up for herself. This time, however, the words wouldn't come. Somewhere, in her head, that voice that usually broke forth at times like this was too exhausted to find the words. Her gaze drifted down to her black, flat shoes. They were more comfortable than heels but not as comfortable as trainers. She probably only had around thirty minutes left by now, once she got out of here she could swap the shoes for the trainers in her bag. As she shifted, her trouser leg lifted, showing off black sock underneath.

She had to pack her son's socks. Would he have enough? Of course he would, the boy hated wearing socks. Where did he get that from?

85

'Sue's off sick today, you know?' came Graham's voice.

'Hmm, I heard.' Wendy had fond memories of wearing thick, fluffy socks in winter, sitting by the open fire of the Manor. Her father would ask her if her feet were too hot, that she should move or take the socks off, but she never wanted to do either so she'd lie and say she was fine.

'Flu, she thinks. She'll be off the rest of the week, so we probably won't see her again until the New Year,' said Graham.

'Oh, that's a shame.' Sure, sitting with sweaty toes wasn't pleasant but her son was rarely sitting in front of a fire wearing thick, fluffy socks. Still, he always complained his feet were too hot. Were her feet always too hot? She wiggled her toes in her shoes.

'Which rather throws the Christmas fair into a dilemma,' said Graham. 'She was organising it with one of our juniors. He kindly volunteered to help.'

Her toes didn't feel hot. The action of wiggling them reminded her of being warm, in bed. A wave of exhaustion washed over her.

'And, of course, we can't cancel the fair. It's on in a week and so important to our reputation. The marketing team have already done the PR. All those people we don't want to disappoint.'

He must get it from his father, Wendy decided. Her ex-husband had always had hot feet in bed. She'd loved it when they'd first gotten together. For a while there, right at the beginning, he'd let her warm her cold feet on him during the winter nights. Something in Wendy's chest ached.

'So, we need a new volunteer to organise the Christmas fair and I realised I know just the person. You, Wendy. So, I'll introduce you to James and you can get acquainted. Yes?'

There was a pause. A silence that filled the room and infiltrated Wendy's thoughts. She blinked and looked up.

'Sorry?'

'You'll finish organising the Christmas fair with James,' said Graham.

Wendy was certain there was a question mark missing.

'I have a pretty heavy caseload at the moment, Graham.'

'Sue's already done most of the organising. It won't take you much time. And there's only a week to go. It'll be over before you know it. And you said you're ready for Christmas, kids aren't with you, so less to prepare, right?'

'That's not really—'

'The Christmas fair is on Friday afternoon. We're making our final decision about who becomes partner at the end of Friday. Right before we close for the year. So once the fair is over, you can go home, grab your bags and head to your brother's. What a great way to finish the year.'

Wendy hesitated, her tired mind desperately trying to work out why he'd slipped in the part about the promotion.

'Graham.'

'I've already checked your cases. Nothing's closing this week. You should be fine.'

'Graham, does my organising this fair have any impact on whether I get the promotion?'

Another pause, this one heavier than the last as Graham's eyes lifted to meet hers.

'Of course not,' he told her. 'We couldn't do that.'

Wendy let the silence fill the room until Graham smiled.

'I'll introduce you to James now, shall I?'

She blinked.

'James?'

'The junior who'll be helping you. He was helping Sue. He'll catch you up and you can delegate to him. See, I told you it'd be easy.'

'Graham—'

He was already up, walking towards the door and beckoning for Wendy to follow. Once out in the main open office, she could hardly raise her voice and make accusations, so she followed silently. This was an opportunity to gather her thoughts, which is why her eyes were down and she nearly bumped into Graham when he stopped.

'James, this is Wendy Winshaw—'

'Hargreaves.'

'Hmm?'

'I've reverted to my maiden name,' said Wendy, still trying to corral some logical, sensible thoughts.

'Right. This is Wendy Hargreaves, one of our senior associates. She'll be taking over from Sue. I want you to catch her up and help her in any way you can. Let's make this fair a great one.' Graham grinned at them both.

Wendy finally lifted her gaze, looking from Graham to this junior called James. He wasn't what she'd been expecting. When she'd heard "junior" she'd conjured up a mental image of a young person, perhaps in their early twenties, straight out of university. This man could pass for late twenties but there was something about him that screamed thirties. Something grown up, something more mature, a certain look about his dark eyes. While the other juniors wore suit jackets, James had removed his and rolled his sleeves up. His arms were muscular and covered with thick, dark hair. That was not something Wendy should have been noticing. She looked back up into those dark eyes and he smiled at her, holding out a hand.

'Pleasure to be working with you,' he said in a smooth voice. He was clean shaven but the afternoon was becoming late and stubble was already making its way back to his chin. He smelled of coffee but there was still a whiff of cologne or aftershave about him.

'And you,' said Wendy, all rational, logical thoughts so carefully processed on the walk over were forgotten. She shook his hand and he gave hers a small squeeze that twisted her stomach. She tried to blink the feelings away.

'Excellent,' said Graham. 'I'll leave you two to it.'

Wendy opened her mouth to protest but Graham had already left, finding someone to drag with him in a loud conversation so she couldn't call him back.

'You sod,' she muttered.

'What's that?'

Wendy turned back to James and attempted a smile.

'Nothing. Nothing.'

'Okay.' James cleared his throat, looking away. 'Do you want to go through the fair plans now?' He looked back to his desk.

Wendy pulled her phone from her pocket and checked the time. She sighed.

'Sorry, I have to dash. Can we do it first thing tomorrow? When do you get in?'

'Eight.'

Wendy blinked. Eight in the morning. She remembered what she used to be able to get into the office at eight in the morning. In the days before the children. In the days before the husband, even.

'Okay, half nine?' she asked. 'Let's get together and go through it then.'

James nodded.

'Sure. Half nine tomorrow.'

There was an awkward pause as James sank back into his chair and Wendy realised she was standing there for no good reason.

'Right. Great. Thanks. See you then.' She swiftly turned on her heel and marched away, her chest and cheeks burning. She wiggled her toes as she walked and there it was, a bit of sweat. She almost laughed. As if she had time right now for butterflies in her stomach and staring at men who might possibly be quite attractive. Christmas was in just over a week, her workload had potentially just doubled and she still had to pack her son's socks.

**

Printed in Great Britain
by Amazon

14248306R00052